A must re [illegible] es.

— *Hon Baka*

Spot on and real.

— *Stella Myers*

Cold Blood not only shows you the beginning of Yamabuki's story as a teenage Samurai, it also contrasts her life to that of the woman she would have been had she not opted to tread the warrior's path. That draws out the best elements of historical fiction.

— *Carlyle Clark, Heroines of Fantasy*

Lawrence's descriptive skills struck me especially. . . . Yamabuki is a wonderful character, and she is coming of age just before a ruinous war in Japan.

— *Anne Vonhof*

I was torn between wanting to race through the story to find out what happened next and wanting to linger over the tale, savoring the exotic and the unusual.

— *C.R.*

Cold Blood

冷血
REIKETSU

Cold Blood

A Yamabuki Story

Sword of the Taka Samurai
Book One

Katherine M. Lawrence

Toot Sweet Ink
tootsweet.ink

Boulder

This is a work of fiction. All of the characters, organizations, and events portrayed in this book are either products of the author's imagination or are used fictitiously. Any resemblance to actual events or locales or persons, living or dead, is purely coincidental.

Book design by Laura Scott

A Toot Sweet Ink Book
Published by Toot Sweet Inc.
6525 Gunpark Drive Suite 370
Boulder, CO 80301

Visit us at tootsweet.ink

Library of Congress Control Number: 2014958564

First Edition

ISBN: 978-0-9912667-1-5 (hardback)

ISBN: 978-0-9912667-2-2 (trade paper)

ISBN: 978-0-9912667-3-9 (ebook)

To LS

Contents

Long before it was called Japan,
the island empire was known
to the world as Akitsushima,
the Autumn Creek Land,
and among its samurai,
one of its mightiest warriors was
a woman named Yamabuki.

Cold Blood

Spring 1172:
Known as Year of the Metal Rabbit,
Second Year of Shōan,
eight years prior to the Genpei War
and the ensuing struggle
for the mastery of Japan
that tore the realm apart
and ushered in the era of the warlords.

One

Blue Rice

4 bell strikes
First quarter, Hour of the Snake
Full Moon of New Life Month

The Kanmon Strait

In pristine battle armor, traveling without her personal guards or handmaids, not wearing any insignia that revealed her exact rank, Yamabuki at last stood in her own right on the promontory that looked north across the Barrier Strait. The rising sun burned so bright that the heavens scarcely looked blue. Shimmering light shone all the way across the vast Windward Sea which flowed off the edge of the world at the eastern horizon.

A moist westerly breeze caressed the warrior's young face, leaving the slightest taste of brine on her lips and the fresh scent of fish and kelp in her nostrils.

Mochizuki, her jet-black two-year-old colt, snorted his displeasure.

"I know you don't like the wind," she whispered, reaching up to stroke his mane with one hand while tightening her grip on his bridle with the other. His hot wet breath blew across her hand.

As with all horses, his hearing was keen and he grew fretful when anything impeded it.

She wondered to what extent his disquiet had infected her. Ever since crossing into Chikuzen Province two days before, her mount had grown increasingly temperamental—possibly because the North Road from Mizuki to Kita had teemed with people, horses, carts, wagons, and livestock. Disguised as a common samurai, more or less blending into the throng, Yamabuki trusted that she had escaped notice. However, if someone was shadowing her, it would have been easy enough for them to meld in as well.

This morning she dismissed her earlier apprehensions as mere fancy and instead looked ahead. She strained to make out the opposite shore through the thin, lingering haze, which washed out the details of the Main Isle of Honshu, her destination.

A voice startled her. "'Better to cross the strait as the sun rises than as she sets.' At least that's how the commoners put it." The voice belonged to a man who not only had the temerity to interject himself into a nonexistent conversation with her, but even had the impertinence to approach her along her horse's opposite flank, the samurai's blindside.

Since Mochizuki stood between her and the stranger, at first all she could see was the man's muddy sandals and loose-fitting cotton trousers, blue-on-white, with the *ine* rice plant pattern.

She immediately stepped around her mount, her left hand near, but not exactly on, her sword hilt. Her eyes met the stranger's.

He's not even armed, let alone warrior class.

He had a ruddy face. Handsome in a rugged way. A bit older than she. Kindly bloodshot eyes which were happy and sad all at the same time.

Odd. A rich man's sandals, but a commoner's tunic.

As he grinned, his eyes smiled. He may have noticed her sword hand. "I was just behind you on the road all the way up from Kita. Wasn't following," he assured. "Just going to the trailhead."

He cast his gaze toward Honshu. "Boatmen call this place Dragon's Throat. It's the shortest distance between the Great Isles. The two seas somehow know it, too, and so they rush through the channel. In the end, the shortest distance to land has the strongest currents."

She moved her hand away from her weapon.

He tossed a wrist in a casual gesture toward the north eastern horizon. "Beautiful morning for it though. We are both crossing the barrier, no?"

Resolute, she looked across the turbid expanse. Seemingly lost in the idea of crossing, finally she answered softly, almost to herself, "I haven't traveled for ten days and nights for just a view."

"Ha-ha!" he laughed, respectfully looking her up and down. "White crossed arrow-feather insignia on indigo. You are of the Taka clan from Great Bay Province . . . from the southeastern tip, yes?"

"As far from here as it is possible to be, yet still be on the same isle."

"*Hai*, but not for long." His eyes narrowed. "Hear that?" He tilted his head, his ear toward the sea.

She found that for the moment she could hear nothing more than the hum of a steady wind mingling with the soft pulse of the sea and the occasional screeches of wheeling gulls. Since her battle helmet concealed her hair gathered up under its steel crown, if she removed her *kabuto* to improve her hearing, her long locks would be released and everyone would immediately see that she was a female, and a young one at that. But then, a moment later, shouts drifted up from the water below.

The man beckoned her to the sea cliff's edge. "My ears aren't actually *that* good," he said, pointing over the side. "I saw the cargo boat enter the cove."

She peered down the nearly vertical drop-off of gray clay and rock. Far below, a festively decorated shallow-draught *kobune*, crammed to capacity with about forty warriors, tacked toward shore. Its *senchou* skillfully guided his craft through the swirling whitish-blue current that streamed out to sea. As he maneuvered the kobune toward the wooden landing, thick rope coils flew from the boat to waiting hands on the shore. In the splendidly open air, the voices of the shore crew's calling-song carried up from below, echoing off the surrounding crescent cliffs.

Haul, haul. Heave-ho! Heave-ho!
Put your backs in. Dokkoisho!
Though the gulls call us
We cannot tarry
Pretty girls we wait to marry
(Please wait, please wait.)

Steadily the haulers drew the craft out of the tidal basin and toward the calmer waters near the decaying timbers of the makeshift dock. Though weathered by salt spray and the pounding sun, and feasted upon by all manner of marine bores, the pier's roughhewn pilings were still sturdy enough for lashing and securing the boat. The lines were hardly tied when the contingent of samurai leapt onto the dock.

"Looks like an invasion," Yamabuki said drolly.

The man in the white-on-blue kimono laughed, for they both knew it was nothing of the kind. The warriors were merely glad that they had reached their destination and could at last escape the wave-tossed kobune. Doubled over on the rocky beach, three of the passengers joined into the ancient and unwelcome ritual of losing the contents of their stomachs.

"They didn't drink enough saké," he breathed.

"For courage?" She looked askance.

"No," he said seriously, "you drink it because it makes the land move like the sea. If you've drunk enough before you board, once you're out on the water, you can't tell the difference. You won't get seasick."

He reached into his copious sleeve, where he dug around until his face brightened. "This one's full." He pulled out an ornate porcelain flask with the ine emblem painted on its side. Raising the saké bottle high, he breathed, "It's what you'll need to cross the barrier."

He hummed, rolling his tongue across his lips.

"Good saké. Strong." He smiled more broadly as he unstoppered the flask and offered the bottle's now naked neck to her.

With a subtle gesture of her small finger, she indicated for him to take it away.

He shook the bottle hard enough that she could hear the saké slosh inside. "If we don't drink together, it will mean you have no friends."

To most people, at least of her class, a person's mouth was considered to be unclean. A vile thing. Contact with another's mouth, or whatever it touched, was unthinkable to all but the most wanton. Even the practice of mouth-sucking was usually confined to the bedchamber, and then only between married people or among lovers.

Yamabuki shook her head.

"I do not have any sickness, if that's what you think," he huffed.

"I'm not thirsty," she replied, her eyes slightly drawn, but expressing a modest smile of politeness.

Far below, the seasick warriors eventually recovered and chased after their fellows, who already were headed up the steep cliff-trail.

"They're Ōuchi clan." He gulped down a generous mouthful of saké and continued, "And low-ranking ones at that."

"And how do you know this?"

"For one, the *hanabishi* insignia on their banner flags. The diamond-flower is the Ōuchi clan symbol."

"That doesn't declare their rank."

"No." He nodded, looking pleased with his own perspicacity, which he celebrated with another swig. "It does not, but that boat carries a horse-blind, yet they don't have a horse amongst them. They even packed some of their number into the kobune's stable." He twisted his nose into a sign of a disgusting smell. "As I said, low ranking. Samurai of importance ride horses. The better the horse, the higher their status," he said, shooting a glance at Mochizuki.

Although he had readily recognized her clan crest, had offered her saké, and had even spoken to her about the "common people," as if they were the "other," the two of them had not exchanged names, nor were they likely to. Such niceties were practiced, of course, only by those of the *buké* warrior class and the *kuge* aristocratic class—in short, among those who had clan affiliations to begin with and therefore had something to announce. Their honored names were derived from being of high rank while in service of a local ruler, or were handed down to the progeny of the various branches of the imperial households.

Even then, disclosing one's names and titles was not done without a specific reason. Such reasons could vary, from forming a lifelong friendship all the way to initiating a duel to the death. In the latter case the combatants would, before ever drawing steel, announce not only their clan and personal names, but their titles and, above all, their impressive string of victories, real or embellished.

But when it came to commoners, what good would it be to exchange names? The upper classes called them *nanigashi*, the thus-and-such people—names such as carpenter, woodcutter, fisherman, *kago* runner, combined with some mundane personal name: Tree, Mountain, River, First Born, Second Born, Young Cattle, and so forth. Hardly worth taking the time to remember.

The man with the saké bottle did not fit into any immediately identifiable commoner category. Still, she was unwilling to exchange names with him, though she wanted to refer to him in some way, if only to herself.

Yamabuki eyed him. Because of his blue kimono with its rice plant pattern, she gave him a sobriquet: *Aoi Ine*. Blue Rice.

He lifted his flask and took a drink. "Sure you don't want any?"

Again Yamabuki politely declined.

With that, Blue Rice turned and moved away from the bluff. "Well then, it shall not be long now. My sister awaits me across the channel. If I don't miss my guess, the senchou will be shoving off soon enough. They never wait for very long." He smiled wistfully.

"I shall see you down to the dock," he said over his shoulder as he walked away.

Yamabuki looked askance. "Not taking the trail?"

"The road."

"That's longer," she called after him.

"Reminiscence," he shouted back and disappeared around the downhill bend.

She looked at the empty road, shaking her head. *I suppose this is how common people speak. Even if Blue Rice thought I was merely of the buké class, his manners are so forward!*

Has he been following me? Not just now—since Mizuki. Maybe even before. Is he aware of the mission I am on?

Whether he was a spy or was not, whether he knew the purpose of her journey or not, there was no turning back.

Yamabuki retightened the binding cords of the straw protecting Mochizuki's hooves, cinched her own helmet cords, took her mount's reins, and headed toward the awaiting kobune.

Two

Wolves Recognizing Wolves

Indeed there were two routes down the cliff. The one Blue Rice took, called Carriage Road, was longer, wider, and more gentle. It consisted of a series of graded switchbacks that could accommodate draft carts, merchant wagons, and the occasional royal carriage. It was the road Yamabuki had always taken before, but unlike Blue Rice, never on foot.

Today, Yamabuki chose the route called Foot Trail. Steeper than Carriage Road, it had the advantage of being more direct and therefore faster. Over the centuries the footfalls of the thousands who had approached the Barrier Strait had carved a steep path into the cliff face. Even so, in too many places the path was still scarcely horse width.

Yamabuki recalled advice from the previous evening when, in the commoner's manner of speaking, innkeeper Inu had described the manners, protocol, and nuances she could expect at the channel crossing point, explaining it thus: If the weather was seasonable and the tides right, travelers with means could find boats of assorted sizes, with captains of varying skill, to ferry passengers, livestock, horses, carts, and cargo. For a fair sum, the boatmen would accommodate just about anyone—regardless of rank—traveling in either direction, no questions asked. Even if someone had a price on his head, with enough additional gold to cover the additional risk (and required bribes), under the cover of darkness the senchou would deliver his passenger to one of the numerous (and discreet) alternate landing spots away from the ever-present spears of the shoreline patrols.

This day marked Yamabuki's fourth crossing to the Main Isle. On the three prior crossings, as a maiden of the Taka House, she had traveled in a grand carriage escorted by a retinue flying Taka clan banners in a stylized journey with its own punctilious practices, including the requirement that each and every commoner who encountered the retinue had to pause, bow down, and pay homage. For as long as there had been written records, this was how the empire's sixty-six provincial *daimyō*, the landholding self-styled warlords, were honored when they traveled.

And, over time, the level of required obeisance had evolved. Centuries had passed since any emperors had ventured beyond the immediate outskirts of Heian-kyō, let alone braved the journey to the southern-most of the empire's four Great Isles. And in the absence of imperial visits, the local daimyō had decided they would afford themselves the same high-level courtesies as the Mikado himself. And, thus, as was the case with the Emperor and His family, commoners were not allowed to see those who rode inside any carriages. The faces of the highborn ladies within the daimyō's circle, especially females of marriageable years, were *never* exposed—not even to their betrothed, and then only on their wedding night. At least that was the theory. In reality, sometimes passions needed quenching long before the nuptials, even if it were with someone other than a husband-to-be.

Theories and realities aside, on Yamabuki's prior crossings of the strait, it had fallen to the retinue to clear the path of riffraff, making sure that the prying eyes of the lowborn were directed elsewhere—usually toward the dirt, foreheads touching the soil.

However, on the previous occasions, Yamabuki and the other highborn ladies traveling in her company, in keeping with the custom, would let one of their arms dangle from behind one of the silk-curtained carriage windows; whose arms and which window remained a matter of changing fashion. With arms appropriately extended, the prevailing breeze would pick up the graceful cut sleeves of the women's lavish brocade kimonos. Thus, the quick of eye could catch a glimpse of a milky-white exposed wrist. At this a gasp might escape from someone who kowtowed by the roadside—a muted gasp at that, for if discovered, the wrath visited by the retinue on the offender was swift and painful. Everyone knew firsthand, or at least in the telling, that being smacked with swords, even those still in their scabbards, left bruises.

Men—as men are, from the lowest to the highest—could not help but wonder what fetching creatures remained hidden behind the colorful curtains; and the women for their part laughed and giggled coyly, adding to the allure which their station demanded that they uphold at all times.

Today, however, the demands on Yamabuki were entirely different. Not giggling. Not hiding behind silk curtains nor exposing a wrist. Not in the finest brocade but in the best-made battle gear, she led Mochizuki down Foot Trail while the arriving Ōuchi men trekked up. Her armor covered almost every bit of her body—feet, legs, torso, shoulders, head, arms, and hands—all except for her fingertips, where tactile sense was needed to effectively wield her weapons. And in a twist of irony, the only other part of her flesh that was exposed was her quite naked face.

Yamabuki's personal servants had been aghast that she would let herself be seen thus. Exposed to everyone! Her handmaids had almost insisted, though it was not really their place to do so, that she wear a *mempo* battle mask to conceal her physiognomy.

Nakagawa had suggested otherwise. A mask would only invite curiosity. He had noted there was a common samurai protocol used to defuse unwarranted suspicion: while passing one another on any given street or road, warriors would briefly trade momentary glances in what Nakagawa called the peaceable practice of wolves recognizing wolves.

Though at first she did not care for the custom, quickly she had learned that if another samurai's gaze lingered, she had to look directly back without exactly locking eyes until they looked away in feigned disinterest.

If anything, it was the spirited horse, and not of the seemingly ordinary Taka warrior in the dark-green armor with cobalt-blue woven-silk cords, that drew the attention of other warriors.

During prior journeys, the retinue had forced everyone to gather along the roadside and thus attracted a great deal of mandated attention, after which the retinue thrashed those who could not help but finally look.

But now in the guise of a buké she realized that most people simply moved through the world. Anyone who dared to meet her gaze could apprehend her countenance—though so far on her journey few commoners had.

Though her gear was immaculate, it was not all that different from the gear worn by the warriors now coming up Foot Trail. Like them, she too bore swords, bow, arrows, and a pole arm, as well as the other armaments, such as daggers and throwing stars, peculiar to warriors.

However, there was one thing that might have drawn attention to her, if the others only knew: she carried three scroll-length dispatches hidden on her person. Meant only for the Taka courtiers in Heian-kyō, under no circumstances were they to fall into unintended hands.

Three

The One-Eyed Daimyō of Ten-Legged Things

Yamabuki was more than halfway down Foot Trail when she saw a man whose black hair glistened strangely, almost blue in the sun. Clad in fisherman's gear, on hands and knees, he struggled to recover a tipped-over basket-load of spider crabs that scrambled in every direction. Muttering plaintively about not making it to market on time, one by one he tossed the feisty still-living creatures back into the carrier.

Yamabuki paused while the procession of approaching Ōuchi stepped around the crabber, paying him no more notice than a river would to a large boulder. She watched him moving crab-like. *The daimyō of things ten-legged*, she thought to herself.

Already on his knees, he kowtowed even further, if such a thing were possible. After all, she led a battle horse who needed a wide berth, yet she did not drive the old man off the side of the hill as would have been her warrior-class right.

When he finally did look up, she saw the frayed, thick, and soiled patch he wore over his right eye. He smiled cautiously.

Despite the missing eye, he seemed otherwise fit. He even had all his teeth, which was unusual for a commoner of his years.

"Eating crabs must be bringing you health," she said with a grin. As she moved away from the cliff to walk around the crabber, Mochizuki snorted.

Without warning, an Ōuchi samurai with the build of an ox marched downhill past the temperamental steed, well-nigh knocking the crabber aside. Paying not the least mind to the common fisherman, nor his catch, the samurai tramped straight through the still-swarming crabs. Annoyed by the crab basket in the road, he growled and kicked it, sending more crabs flying.

"Ahh!" The old man let out a muffled scream.

Crunch.

The samurai's foot crushed one crab.

Crunch.

Another crab suffered the same fate.

What impertinence! Yamabuki stiffened at the affront to her, not the crabber.

The samurai moved as if he could not get to the dock fast enough. She speculated that he must have forgotten something on the boat. But when she saw his sword blade's length, she knew he was definitely not among the Ōuchi warriors who had just come up the hill. She would have certainly remembered someone hefting a field-sword—a weapon whose chief function was to enable foot soldiers to bring down mounted samurai. Too long to sling from the waist, its bearer had to shoulder the *nodachi* blade in the manner of a spear. In fact the amount of steel residing in the blade made it unusually heavy, so much so that it ordinarily took two warriors simultaneously grasping the hilt to correctly swing a field sword through its effective arc. However, if a warrior possessed exceptional strength, he might master one-man-nodachi-style, enabling him to hack down any adversary before his opponent could ever get close.

Momentarily her thoughts flashed back to the day Nakagawa had brought his own nodachi into the Taka training hall back in Great Bay Province and challenged her, his ten-year-old student at the time, to find a way to defend against it. *"For the very strong,"* he had said, *"a nodachi provides many advantages, yet a weakness is buried in each."* But, as always, he never exactly showed her the answer, and of course he never revealed it in words. But after a score of days in the training hall had passed, she came to understand how to defeat the nodachi: *speed.*

She continued to watch as the long-sword samurai disappeared around a switchback. *So,* she thought to herself, *this "Long Sword" will likely have to be endured on the boat today.* She frowned.

The fisherman, still on all fours, chased after what remained of his catch.

She moved on, leaving him to his woes.

But the one-eyed man was watching her retreating back, and once she was around the bend and barely out of sight, he leapt up and started scaling the hillside, abandoning his crabs and basket in the middle of the trail.

Climbing like a goat, he reached an overlook point in a line of sight with the beach.

He pulled a bright yellow silk scarf out of his tunic. Raising it high, he let the prevailing wind catch it. When the scarf started to flutter, he waved it frantically.

Moments later, in answer, a mirror glint flashed up from the beach.

With that he stuffed the yellow shawl back into his tunic and clambered even higher up the rocky hillside, disappearing into the pines, leaving the ten-legged things to their own devices.

Four

Full Moon Tide

Yamabuki arrived at the base of Foot Trail. The sun had risen high enough to wash the cove with full morning light, but beneath the bluff's semi-shadow, by the water's edge where the air was definitely cooler, squawking gulls scuttled across the rocks, sand, and shell. Out in the channel cormorants and pelicans poked their bills into dark waters, coming up with prey in their beaks.

Up and down the shore, villagers with waterlogged wooden buckets dug around the half submerged larger boulders. *Oyster hunters.*

She looked further along the shoreline to the point where the land curved away from the channel, beyond which only the wide-open, mysterious blue ocean stretched toward the world's edge.

Near land's end she noticed a small hovel. Dirty smoke rose from a vent in the roof. Someone had notched together a series of square wooden frames. They lay on the sand just outside the hut. *Probably salt makers.*

Standing on some rocks above a tidal pool, two laughing young men with shaven heads, flowing white robes, and thick walking sticks skipped pebbles out into the channel to see who could get the most hops over the wave tops of the rapidly outgoing tide. *Buddhists. Tendai sect, no doubt.*

She saw the samurai with the nodachi sitting on a large boulder high above the water, away from everyone else. He had assumed the countenance of a rotund Buddha, but instead of gold-plate, this one sat clad in indigo armor. He scowled as he studied the two monks.

Well, she laughed to herself, *almost a Buddha. A scowling Buddha at best. Hmm. What interest does he have in the monks? A manly attraction? Maybe. They certainly could be pleasing.*

One of the oyster hunters, a reedy girl with a sweet smile, carefully approached Yamabuki. The girl glanced uneasily at Mochizuki, who for the moment remained placid. Overcoming whatever fear she might have had, the girl lifted a brimming bucket for Yamabuki's inspection.

"Oysters, samurai-sama?" she said, bowing.

Yamabuki had not eaten an oyster since she left the shores of Great Bay Province, and the mere sight of the barnacle-covered shells filled her with memories of home.

"How much?" Yamabuki asked.

"A copper," the girl answered, casting her eyes down.

Yamabuki's eyes narrowed. "A copper? For how many?"

The girl started. Her eyes shot back up. Her lips quavered slightly.

The older oyster hunters, who waded out among the rocks, watched the interchange from out of the corners of their worried eyes.

Likewise, Yamabuki watched the oyster hunters.

Their fear was obvious, and she understood their concern. Both she and they knew that most samurai made a point of being unpredictable, temperamental, and dangerous. A samurai would think nothing of striking an oyster hunter, whatever her age, who delivered an insult, real or imagined.

Trying to stay only a bit stern, Yamabuki glanced at the bucket. "Are they good? Fresh?"

"Just now," the girl answered, pointing back toward the oyster hunters who waded ever further out into the channel. "Full Moon tide. Water's low. Good."

Yamabuki looked skeptically into the bucket. When she let her eyes meet the girl's, she did not show her samurai face. She smiled down at the child. "They alive?"

"Hai," the girl replied and poked her finger into the various open shells, each of which lazily closed.

"One copper. Five oysters."

The girl's eyes opened wide.

Maybe she can't count. Yamabuki held up five fingers.

The girl bowed very low.

Humph. Looks like I've already agreed to pay too much.

The girl quickly fished out five oysters, ones toward the bucket bottom.

"These're the best," she said, catching her breath. "Biggest. Freshest of all."

The girl yanked a knife out of her sash and shucked the five with total alacrity, setting the half shells on a waist high boulder next to Yamabuki.

Large indeed. Yamabuki took the closest oyster and lifted it, shell and all, to her lips to scoop the meat off into her mouth; she could not help but smile as the taste of ocean mingled with the delicate flavor of the oyster's flesh.

Yamabuki handed the girl the promised copper.

The girl scurried away to the other oyster gatherers, where there was much talking, nodding of heads, and veiled gesturing in Yamabuki's direction.

Indeed, I definitely paid too much. Still, as she finished the fifth and final oyster, it tasted just as good as the first. In fact, it was better than what she remembered being served at her estate house in the Taka compound.

Maybe the old saw was true: *"Oysters taste best when your toes touch the sea."*

She was sated. The copper coin was irrelevant, the actual purchase being the girl's momentary smile.

One more thing remained. She reached into her saddle pouch to remove a small bamboo canteen adorned with an indigo-black jade Taka crest. She took a quick, yet ample, sip of saké from the flask innkeeper Inu had replenished just that morning. *Not too much, now*, she reminded herself. *Who knows how long it will be before I again shall taste saké such as this?*

Just then she heard sounds behind her that echoed and re-echoed along the crescent cliffs: a group of shouting men coming down the Carriage Road. She counted six of them. They rolled a rickety two-wheel cart onto the rocky beach. All wore vivid green work tunics decorated with golden roundels. Fine clothes or not, the men wrestled like common laborers with the handcart they had stacked to overflowing with bundles.

They are wearing fine fabrics. Probably fabric merchants.

One of their number, who seemed to be the master weaver, animatedly pointed, bobbed his head, and waved his arms. The other men heaved, pulled, and shouted at one another, but finally the cart bumped its way over the rocks and onto the wide set of planks that covered the last forty or so strides to the dock. Even so, the merchants were making painfully slow progress.

For the time being, Yamabuki thought it best to keep her colt back from their ruckus.

She glanced back at Carriage Road and saw Blue Rice saunter onto the beach. He paused. Taking in a deep breath, he placed one hand up to shield his face from the direct rays of the sun, which just now broke over the highest top of the hillside.

"Feed for your handsome stallion, samurai-sama?" asked a wizened man, stooped from carrying a load of hay across his back. "Only one copper for *all* this."

A copper for just *that? Then again, Mochizuki won't eat that much anyway; and besides, it will keep him quiet.*

She flipped the man the coin, which he caught one-handed. He set the bale down, bowed, and scurried away. Mochizuki snorted and immediately started to munch.

The sun was still rising. She turned her gaze toward the mid-morning seascape, taking in the beauty, wishing to seal these precious moments in her memory.

It would be some time before she would cross home over Barrier Strait.

The morning moon had set. Though she did not wish to let herself become overly sentimental, her Taka-born characteristic realism reminded her that sentimentality might *not* be an indulgence at all.

As the tide moved out to sea, she felt a sweeping sense of *awaré*, the sorrowful awareness that the world is transient.

Five

The Boyish Face Behind the Mask

THE PRIOR AFTERNOON, JUST as the sun had begun to settle into the Leeward Sea, Yamabuki had ridden into the bustling coastal port of Kita, a town of a thousand strangers. Only a quarter hour's ride from the Barrier Strait, the town consisted more or less of two hundred permanent structures, including several inns, making it the perfect place for travelers to bed down and wait for the dawn.

As was the custom among the Taka, she sought out the Inn of Young Bamboo, the Wakatake. A place of genuine hospitality, the inn was a source of valuable information to the Taka as to what and who of note passed by on the road, as well as sailed into and out of the port. The Yūkū family, Wakatake's fifth-generation proprietors, were not only friendly to the Taka but also in the clan's pay.

Don't the Taka call innkeeper Inu "Ears"?

Yamabuki stopped Mochizuki in front of the inn and took a moment to observe the surroundings.

A chest-high fence of woven bamboo staves separated the front garden from the street, but it did not obstruct the inviting view of the large building, one of the few two-story structures in all of Kita. Emerald banners inscribed with white calligraphy flew to tout the inn to passersby. A wide first-floor veranda ran the inn's entire perimeter. Heavy wooden outer doors stood open to let in the warm and fragrant spring afternoon.

She slung her leg over the saddle and, despite wearing full armor, leapt down, landing gracefully and solidly on her feet. She tethered Mochizuki at the entry gate, taking in the sweet aroma of the cherry blossoms that bloomed in abundance.

No sooner had she set foot through the gateway than Old Inu stepped out onto the veranda.

"Welcome, Lady Taka. Welcome!" Having not aged a day, he almost sprang on the balls of his feet, bowing low several times as he approached her. "I was told you might be our guest tonight, though I wasn't exactly sure when you were going to arrive."

She indicated with a small gesture of her hand that he should not so freely reveal her exact identity.

"Ha!" he exclaimed, blushing a bit from embarrassment. "Don't worry. You're our only guest tonight. No one else's here. I've been telling everyone that we have no rooms."

Then she noticed a stranger hanging back in the entryway shadows. Quite tall, at least as tall as she. Powerful of build, he stood erect like a warrior.

"You said *I* was the only guest." She pointed in the stranger's direction.

"Ah?" Inu's breath caught in his throat. Immediately he spun his head to where she pointed, but then he exhaled slowly as he turned back to her with a satisfied expression. "Ahhh!" Inu scoffed politely, waving the so-called stranger forward. "Have you forgotten him? That's Ryuma!"

Ryuma? Her memory flashed back four years to the willowy stable boy she had known. If this were truly he, that boy had filled out and grown handsome—virile in fact, though she could still see the boyish face behind the mask of the man he had become.

Inu bowed to acknowledge Ryuma's presence. "I suppose he's grown since you were last here, but then, if I am permitted to say, so have *you*. He's now become, how shall I say this, an *assistant*."

"Assistant? Assistant of what?"

"Oh," Inu began vaguely, "he's helpful where a young man's strength's needed. Say that someone comes to the inn and becomes violent. Or, say that a guest decides not to pay. Ryuma helps them remember the rules."

"He's your hatchet man then, is he?"

"At least that," Old Inu said, and added slyly, "and he performs other duties as well. Come. No need to stand here. The sun has already begun to set." Inu bowed low.

Yamabuki inclined her head. "My mount."

"Ryuma," said Inu. "Her horse."

Ryuma stepped further out onto the veranda and met Yamabuki's eyes. For a moment an expression of something unspoken flitted across his face.

She held his gaze for as long as protocol required, but he turned his eyes away before it was time and bowed.

Why is he so dour?

"Take her horse to the back," Inu commanded in a light tone.

"His name is Mochizuki," she said waiting to see if Ryuma would look at her again.

He passed her without glancing at her. "His name, then, is Full Moon?" Ryuma muttered barely above a whisper.

"Just under two years old and still half wild. Can you manage him?" Yamabuki chided gently with a smile. "Don't be afraid to ask for help, if you need it. Mochizuki can be a handful."

"I can," he said. "Not my first encounter with half-wild things," he breathed, his back to her. Confidently he took Mochizuki's reins and, still not looking at Yamabuki, led the mount to the back.

Yamabuki, her eyes narrowed, watched Ryuma walk away.

"Come." Inu stepped onto the veranda, beckoning her spiritedly. "I'll get everything prepared," he said, after which he disappeared inside.

She followed him through the entry.

Just inside, two fetching female attendants waited with gracious smiles. Several years younger than she, the girls were dressed in fine silk kimonos: one in peach, the other in straw green. The two girls bowed politely, and then straightaway started to remove Yamabuki's battle gear, untying its disparate fastenings. The two girls were well aware of the protocol and the stacking of arms, which they accomplished with a minimum of conversation. Efficiently they slipped off her shoulder plates, untied her corselet armor, and lifted away her sleeve protectors, placing all the pieces just inside the door on a small stand that had been built for just this purpose.

They took her *tachi*, which she had named Tiger Claw, and placed it, scabbard and all, on a weapons rack, but not her shorter personal sword, Tiger Cub, which they left with her. The final piece of her armor to come off was, as custom would have it, her kabuto; but when they loosened its binding cords from her chin and lifted the helmet free, Yamabuki's hair immediately spread out and fell to her shoulders.

"Oh, so *long*," whispered the girl in peach, stressing her words to show her awe.

The girl in the straw-green kimono tittered.

"You are *pretty!*" exclaimed the girl in peach, her eyes dancing in genuine surprise as they met Yamabuki's.

"I trust you will keep *that* a secret," Yamabuki replied under her breath. "What is your name?"

"I'm Ishi-tsuki."

"And you?" Yamabuki asked the girl in straw green.

"I'm Chi-ye."

"Ah. Stone Moon and Thousand Blessings."

Yamabuki stood in her own dark-green outer kimono with its embroidered gold turtle-back pattern, and her matching *hakama*, a split-trouser riding-skirt usually worn only by the upper class. She slipped Tiger Cub through her kimono's cobalt-blue waist sash.

"My lady," Ishi-tsuki said with some astonishment. "You're still dressed like a samurai."

Yamabuki replied, "That's good." She paused. "Because I *am* a samurai."

Ishi-tsuki blushed, and her hands shot to her cheeks to cover the fact.

No longer able to keep a straight face, Yamabuki laughed. Chi-ye joined in.

Old Inu reappeared at the entry. "Come. Food. Saké. Songs. Dancing."

Inu bowed, leading Yamabuki further inside Wakatake where

he bade her sit. She took her place, that of honor, before a low table, placing Tiger Cub on the floor to her right, in easy reach.

The staff had readied cold, strong saké and steaming white rice mixed with seaweed, as well as a plate of slow-cooked young boar. She had not eaten this well in several days, and as the old saying went, "*Every food is delicious to a hungry man*"; yet she knew the difference: Inu's rice and seaweed was superb, the boar succulent, and his cold saké strong and pure.

Inu slipped away for a brief moment, then returned bearing a black-lacquered bamboo serving plate with raw, freshly cleaned fish elegantly laid out down to the tiniest detail.

"*Fugu.*" Inu grinned as he moved his arm in a flourish, inviting her to partake. "A delicacy from these waters."

"Fugu?" She looked askance, for puffer fish had a dubious reputation. If properly cleaned and prepared, it was said to be exquisite. However, since many parts of the puffer were highly poisonous, if the fish were ineptly cleaned, ingesting even the slightest trace was a death sentence.

Six

Raw Courage

YAMABUKI WAS NO MORE than six years of age when she had unwillingly witnessed the fugu toxin at work. During her second stay in Heian-kyō, one of her father's bodyguards, his name was Giichi, touched his tongue to a piece of puffer. His death had been almost immediate. There was a great commotion among the retinue, but no one could do anything for him, for there was no antidote.

From that day forward, fugu was banned from the Take compound. No one was allowed to partake of it. Strictly forbidden! There were more meaningful reasons to die.

She now looked into Inu's hopeful face and then at the colorless fish. "I don't believe that I've ever had the pleasure."

"Hai, fugu. Fresh." Inu bowed. "I prepared it myself. Very good."

Yamabuki paused for the briefest of moments. *Has Inu been informed of my father's decree about Taka not eating fugu?*

Inu, in what in any other circumstances would have been a severe breach of etiquette when serving a guest, especially of her rank, plucked a piece of fugu from the platter and put the morsel into his mouth. "Hmmm." He pressed his lips closed, expressing his enjoyment.

"You have the courage of a samurai . . . and the graciousness of a scrupulous host," she said softly, ready to take a small portion of fugu for herself. The fish was sliced so thin, she could almost see through it.

For a brief moment, her memory again drifted back to what had happened when the tainted fugu had hardly touched Giichi's lips. It was not as if Giichi was just one of her father's numerous guards. She had liked him the way a child likes a beloved uncle, and so it was terrifying to witness Giichi's crash to the floor. She remembered the alarm that had filled his eyes as his breath caught in his throat. Moments later his heart no longer pumped. Giichi's eyes remained wide to the end. All these years later, her own shrieks of horror still rang in her ears.

She took a deep breath. With two wooden *hashi* sticks, she lifted a piece of fish, holding it against the light. It looked like a wafer of ice with the consistency of the most-finely cut radish. She politely placed the piece into her mouth. Her lips closed, her tongue touching the flesh, her teeth biting into the meat.

Immediately an unfamiliar taste filled her mouth. Not what she expected. Not poison, but a delicacy it was not. Bland, in fact. It did not taste nearly as good as her favorite, *buri*, which always tantalized her palate.

Fugu: Tough. Chewy. Like jellyfish.

"Haaaa. Good! Delicious, no?" Inu nodded vigorously, smiling in the triumph of his culinary skills.

Yamabuki mused to herself. *Perhaps the only reason to eat* raw *fugu was to show* raw *courage.*

She exhaled. "Delicious!"

She indicated with her hand that she wished to share it with everyone. "A delicacy," she repeated, and the serving staff, after the polite ritual of several perfunctory refusals required of those with good manners, eagerly partook. Only Ryuma, hatchet man that he was, forbore, keeping his eye on the entries to the room.

After the puffer fish was eaten down to the last bite, seven more young women, all comely, entered the room to serve Yamabuki, bringing her more food bowls, this time filled with an assortment of pickled vegetables, and, of course, more saké flasks.

Though the young women served food and drink, their real purpose was to provide the evening's entertainment: Two of their number brought in string instruments. One carried a drum. And to Yamabuki's surprise, one even played a flute, though the latter was considered the province of men. Three of the other girls were singers.

It was then that Ishi-tsuki and Chi-ye moved to the center of the room.

Seven

In the Battlefield or in Dancing; A Master of Movement

All at once the music began. There may have been only four instruments and three singers, but the room filled with music as grand as at the Taka compound.

Old Inu joined the three singers in an unfamiliar melody. Ishi-tsuki and Chi-ye displayed energy and elegance; their arms and legs moved fluidly in time to the rhythm of the song.

Watching what appeared to be effortless gliding and leaping, Yamabuki could not help but be pleased. She knew the strength and stamina it took to make it look simple.

They performed dance after dance—some animated, some quiet, others with bawdy refrains, but always with feminine grace, even when the steps grew wild and driving.

The last time Yamabuki had been entertained at Wakatake, she was hardly twelve springs; and she had been seated in the second row of the Taka, and then in a separate room at that, for with the retinue of overflowing numbers, several rooms were needed to delight and feed so many.

And it was the retainers who enjoyed the most salacious of the dances.

She, on the other hand, as always, had found herself relegated to the room where girls' songs were sung to the well-bred young ladies. Since girls' songs were mostly soft, at the time she had sometimes caught some of the more raucous refrains and coarse lyrics coming from afar.

But tonight she was the only guest and everyone sat in the same room. She was the focus of everything.

Either because of this newfound freedom, or because she was under sway of the saké—which Ryuma now served while the young women danced—a plan began to form.

Yamabuki declared, "The dances of the Chikuzen District are filled with such energy."

"Oh no," all the girls corrected almost at once, "these are the *toi* dances. Not even of Kita, but of the local fishing settlements."

Yamabuki rose. "Unknown dances of toi? Then you shall have to teach them to me so I may show everyone in Great Bay. So they can realize that the Kita girls' performances are the most magnificent."

Everyone squealed their delight as Yamabuki took her place next to Ishi-tsuki and Chi-ye. They showed her one dance, then another, and another, until she had memorized five in all.

All the while, Yamabuki's saké and food bowls were filled and then refilled to overflowing.

"You might be dressed like a samurai, but you dance like a lady," said Ishi-tsuki. Chi-ye and the others nodded in hearty agreement.

Inu slapped the floor. "Ha! See how a *samurai* moves—in the battlefield or in dancing, she's a master of movement!"

The chamber erupted with approving laughter.

Ishi-tsuki wondered aloud, "Are these dances all so different from Great Bay Province's?"

Yamabuki answered, "They are similar, but they are not exactly the same."

Soon everyone began to beg Yamabuki, "Would you show us the dances of Great Bay Province, then?"

Yamabuki paused thoughtfully, then answered deliberately. "Under two conditions."

All eyes stayed fixed on her.

"First, you have to join in and learn the steps."

Everyone eagerly agreed.

"Then," she continued, "please find me a silk kimono that will fit someone as tall as me!"

"Hai!" Chi-ye bolted up. "I know right where there's one." She immediately returned, handing Yamabuki an elegant kimono of vivid blue heavy silk with finely stitched red cranes and a yellow fine silk inner lining.

Yamabuki unabashedly slipped out of her warrior's garb and into the costume of a lady.

"And now for the music." Yamabuki's face grew serious, yet still cheerful. She hummed a tune.

"Ha. Ha!" the four musicians exclaimed. They knew the song. They began to play the instruments, and the three singers joined in with verses about soft fragrant spring blossoms.

Yamabuki waved her hands. "No. No. We have different words for this song. You just play," she said to the musicians. "You? Clap along," she said to the singers. "And *I*," she paused, "shall sing the verses."

"Do you need a fan?" Chi-ye asked.

With a small smile Yamabuki shook her head as she reached into her warrior's tunic, which had been set aside.

"I shall use mine."

With the snap of her wrist (that of a fancy lady, or was it of a swordsman?) Yamabuki opened her personal *tessen*. Its significance was not lost on anyone in the room. Not only was this her personal iron-ribbed fan, it was also her war fan. Its seventeen folds denoted her rank. Lower ranks had fewer ribs. The Mikado's was twenty-five, the highest allowed in the empire. No one dared carry a fan of more ribs than their rank allowed.

Her tessen, besides doubling as a weapon, was also a symbol of her authority, which meant that despite her youth, she was allowed to command troops in the field. It was said that all she had to do was to raise it in battle and the Taka would rally to her.

Now all anyone needed to do was to politely watch her dance.

Moments later she dropped her noble born manner of speech and began to sing in the thick and all-but-incomprehensible accent that was spoken by the common people of Great Bay, and which few outsiders of any social class could fathom. This made the song sound all the more glamorous.

Yamabuki could not help but notice that Ryuma kept his eyes on her almost every moment.

Is it that he is charmed by me, she wondered to herself, *or is he after something else?*

She smiled enigmatically.

Then with the most gentle, subtle, slow, and soft motions of her arms and hands, she depicted the ocean waves. It was a dance and song about the tide coming in and covering everything that had once been visible, and yet it was a song as much about fate as it was about the sea.

Moments before, everyone had been laughing raucously, but now a hush fell over the room. Only the music, Yamabuki's singing, and the rustle of the kimono could be heard. The sound of the silk was as much a part of the song as were the strings and her voice. *Hishhh. Hishhh.* The silks of the kimono brushed against one another, making the hissing sound of waves coming to shore.

Ascending overhead, over the south
The Sun Goddess shimmers within the sea
The Wind God fetches the breeze
The Sea God drives the waves
In awe we ride the ripples of our fleeting lives
In this world of woe

Tears formed in the corners of Yamabuki's eyes and in the eyes of her audience.

When the last note was plucked, everyone softly murmured, "Good. Very good. How beautiful."

Inu choked back his emotions, forcing a congenial smile. "Ahhh! Lady Taka made us all promise we would learn the dance, too." He leapt to his feet, slapped his knee, which created a more festive mood, commanding, "We must not disappoint!"

With that, Inu, the singers, and the dancers moved forward to join in step—all but the musicians, who continued to play, and Ryuma, who saw to it that Yamabuki's saké bowl stayed full.

She danced, exchanging a glance or two with Ryuma. But she did not permit herself any more eye contact than that. Her focus had to stay fixed on the precise dance steps and the three scrolls she had carefully slipped into her silk kimono sleeve, hidden along with her dagger.

Eight

Someone of the Sex of *Her* Choosing

A coastal front blew in, and the night grew darker and cooler. Yamabuki announced, given all the food, dancing, singing, that it finally was time for her to retire. Everyone expressed disappointment, moaning that the lovely evening was coming to an end far too soon.

Holding an oil brazier, Inu led Yamabuki along the dim hallway, then up a stair ladder. He stopped just outside a chamber that faced the front street.

"Our best room. The backside rooms?" He shook his head. "Too close to the stables."

He slid the screen aside and then, in a voice not much more than a whisper, said, "You will be leaving for the Main Isle tomorrow. Perhaps you would like some companionship, someone to pleasure you on your last night on the Isle of Unknown Fires."

When she raised a brow at the thought of a bed companion, Inu clarified that it would be someone of the sex of *her* choosing, for the Inn of Young Bamboo knew samurai's pleasures were varied.

His inn was in Kita, a crossroads, where *any* accommodation she desired would be met.

If she was in fact tempted by Inu's offer, she did not let on. "Tonight's a time to remember," she said, "not to forget."

He laughed, "Ha! You can do both." He bowed as she entered the chamber.

"I have already selected my *two* companions."

"Two!" Inu's eyes shot up. A look crossed his face. "Ishi-tsuki and Chi-ye?"

"My ink stone and brush."

"Ah," Inu said with a hint of resignation.

"Tonight, I want to think only on my home."

Inu bowed. "Hai." He paused. "But if you should change your mind after you have finished with your ink and brush . . ." He stepped back, slid her chamber door shut, and spoke through the closed door. "If you need anything, call out. We will hear you."

After many hours in others' company, delightful though it was, she sighed with relief that once again she was alone. Maybe because she was still so very young of spirit, Yamabuki would not allow the possibility that this was to be her last crossing of the barrier. How could harm come to her? This would *not* be the last she'd see of the southern-most isle. She *would* come back.

And when she returned to the Taka compound, her diary would be filled with her adventures, the people she met, and what she saw. Nakagawa had encouraged her to observe *everything,* and, while it was still fresh, to set it down in her pillow book.

So instead of seeking distraction in the arms of a stranger, she picked up her brush, which she held with the same confidence as her sword or bow.

Nakagawa had taught her well, from weapons, to mathematics, to language. Few women, especially one just reaching seventeen springs, were allowed to master Hō's calligraphy, let alone were they trained to be fluent in its tongue—Hō, the magnificent kingdom that lay on the furthest edge of the great Leeward Sea.

So on this night, having captured her recollections, but still inspired to write, Yamabuki sat under brazier light to translate a poem composed hundreds of years before by a monk of Hō named Ch'u-mo. His original poem made reference to a monastery on a river. As usual, she translated the calligraphy into the phonetic writing used by literate women of Akitsushima, her own country, or Wa, as it was called by the people of Hō. She dropped several lines of Ch'u-mo's original text, and then, in a dash of boldness, replaced the river he mentioned with the Barrier Strait. This suited her purpose and her mood.

Pleased, she dimmed the brazier and placed the paper aside to let the ink dry.

The town bell struck nine times marking the Third Watch. Somewhere far off a dog barked and then fell quiet.

She lay in the warmth of the bedding, her eyes slowly growing accustomed to the dimness.

The silence was interrupted by the sound of men chanting, "Ho-ha! Ho-ha! Ho-ha!"

She did not need to look. Just listening, she easily pictured the low-class traveling kago with its occupant slung hammock-like in the litter, carried by two runners bearing its support pole over their shoulders. A guide would be running ahead of the kago, calling the pace, carrying a torch to light the way.

Kago. *Deer killer*. She sometimes wondered if the carrier was not named after the poles used by hunters for carrying back wild game, dangling it by its feet.

From their footfalls and voices she could tell that the kago was headed north. "Ho-ha! Ho-ha! Ho-ha!"

But then, the chanting stopped just below her open window.

Behind the partially drawn shutters of the darkened room, she peered down onto the street to get a glimpse of the kago's occupant: a man. She could make out that much, but because the guide's torch was dim and the night was overcast, she could not ascertain the man's age or make out his features.

The kago guide walked into the courtyard, calling loudly, "Innkeeper!"

A stir rippled through the interior of the inn; everyone inside shushed each other, for she, the inn's only guest, was not to be disturbed. Hushed or not, she could hear everything.

"Innkeeper!" the guide cried out again. "An important guest has arrived. Summon your staff."

More sounds floated up from inside the inn. Whispers. Steps. More steps. More than just Inu. The inn's outer door slid aside. Inu's voice reached into the night. "Hai?"

Yamabuki thought Inu's greeting was uninviting, likely because it was meant to be, all without exactly insulting anyone.

"An important guest," the guide repeated.

"Oh, I am *so* sorry. We have *no* rooms left." Yamabuki could picture Inu bowing low.

The man in the kago mumbled something. Yamabuki could not make out the words.

"Then food and drink?" The guide spoke with some agitation.

"Oh, I am *so* sorry," Inu said yet again. "*So* many guests. *So* many appetites. We have nothing left fit for eating or drinking of *important* guests."

"Ha!" the guide almost spat. "It's late! Our passenger is tired."

Another voice from inside the inn rumbled, deep and masculine. It was Ryuma speaking in the tone of a samurai. "Just north of here there're other inns that always have rooms."

"But we have come here," pressed the guide.

Ryuma's voice became almost a growl. "Do you not listen? Other inns can serve you. Up the road, not far at all."

The man in the kago muttered something.

"Sorry to trouble you." The kago guide bowed low toward the inn and turned on his heel and without another word went to the head of the procession.

"Ho-ha! Ho-ha! Ho-ha!" the guide and pole-bearers called out, and the kago and their occupant disappeared into the darkness.

Yamabuki was familiar enough with Kita to know that most all the houses of pleasure were closest to the barrier. Ryuma had directed the stranger there. With their brisk turnover of rooms, vacancies during the night were common, for sleeping was only the secondary purpose of the bedchambers. Anyway, thought Yamabuki, the kago passenger was likely to have a far better time there. This late, most everyone was probably thinking only of lovemaking, and tonight the Inn of Young Bamboo was certainly not a place likely to fulfill a stranger's desires.

Silence fell again.

Lovemaking. She sighed.

A soft rain made itself known on the roof, its sound filling the night.

For a brief moment she wondered if she had been wrong in

refusing companionship. Perhaps the pleasure of someone's company was just the comfort she required. For a moment she imagined herself swept up in another's arms. She imagined the scent. The first touch. The caresses. Then something more.

Should I never return, maybe a last night of love would be . . . Then she thought of Ryuma. *Hmm.* He had not taken his eyes away from her all night, and he had seemed especially attentive when she danced in the silk kimono.

She recalled the intensity of his eyes. The size of his legs. His arms. She wondered how he looked without his kimono. Without anything. Not the spindly boy of four summers ago who had just gone through his *genpuku.*

Back then, Ryuma had been flush with excitement of his coming-of-age celebration, and she, also the same age, had been swept up in the headiness of his mood. Under the guise of checking the horses, he and she had sneaked off together to celebrate his manhood. Yet with his clothes off he had looked as much like a girl as she, except for that *part* of him, or maybe she had looked like a boy, except for *that* part of her. Two sexless would-be lovers who did not know quite what to do, and so they did not do anything.

The memory of that day had faded until now. Yamabuki wondered if thicker hair finally sprouted on his chest? Elsewhere? Probably. He, and certainly she, knew what they could do if only they had the chance to be alone with each other again. Now to her mild surprise her *omeko* grew wet. She tossed.

The rain fell harder. Water sputtered in the downspouts.

Suddenly she realized that she could not rid herself of the image of Ryuma that she had just conjured in her mind.

This is madness. If someone visits my chamber tonight, what then? Word's bound to get back to Great Bay.

The scent of moist wood and thatching filled the chamber. She turned over in her bed, eyes wide, she stared at the ceiling.

Yet Inu had boasted of Wakatake's worldliness. *"Ears" probably would not exactly be in a rush to tell his benefactors how he had not only suggested, but had machinated, that the inestimable Lady Taka would be pleasured in her bedchamber by a man who wasn't her husband.*

She sighed as the rain increased.

But it was more than a matter of what Inu might recount. Servants and retainers insatiably prattled about whom they served. She knew this well for she had seen the same in herself.

Nevertheless, it might be years for the murmurs to reach Great Bay. It might be years before she returned from her errantry.

And if they bring it up, so what?

She sighed deeply, rolled over toward the door, and slid it slightly open.

"Inu?" she called down the hall.

A far-off voice called back, "Yes, my Lady?"

"I want some more saké!"

"Saké? Hai! Saké! I'll be there in a moment."

"Inu?"

"Hai!"

"Can you have Ryuma bring it?"

Nine

Fat Satchels of Coins

Coastal rains can vary, falling in sheets if a storm brews out at sea, or they can be gentle and misty, almost fog-like, if a sea breeze sends in a cloud. It was the latter kind of rain that continued to fall as the kago, its passenger, and its bearers headed ever further into the night. The cloud-shrouded moon offered no help in lighting the way. The running guide raised his torch, holding it as high as he could.

Yamabuki had been wrong in supposing that the kago would wind up at one of the pleasure houses of Kita. Near the edge of town, the kago and runners approached several buildings where feminine voices called out from dimly lit verandas, "Saké. Dancing. Songs. Warm company for the night." But the runners continued right past without missing a step.

As the second bells of the Third Watch rang, marking the end of the first quarter of the Hour of the Mouse, the runners left the main road and entered a grove of fruit trees. Immediately the pole-bearers fell silent. Under thinning torchlight, the kago and bearers headed down a long-forgotten path to a shadowy home, an old-style pit dwelling where an impoverished farmer might live. The sound of rain filled the orchard—drops hitting the fresh flowers and then trickling off. The scent of wet soil, lush blossoms, and salt air floated in the dark. A thin wisp of smoke rose through the roof vent of the shadowy farmhouse.

The kago bearers stopped and slowly lowered the litter. The passenger, shrouded in a dark cloak, stepped out. Fat satchels of coins were handed to the kago runners, who pocketed their earnings and slipped into the night like ninja, headed back to Kita, likely to the pleasure houses.

The shadowy figure stood still in the rain.

Moments later, the door to the house opened a crack. A narrow column of light escaped. A person behind the door asked, "Was the courier at the Wakatake Inn?"

"She was. She had bodyguards. We wait. Too many things could go wrong tonight."

"Then in the morning?"

The cloaked man grunted, stepped into the hut and the door closed. The smoke continued through the night.

Ten

The Ōuchi Samurai

Yamabuki stood on the beach, smiling with memories of Ryuma the previous evening. The struggling fabric merchants' commotion ceased . . . which brought her back to the present. She saw that the boatmen had at last secured the merchants' cart to the kobune deck.

The senchou cried out, announcing to the travelers that the kobune was about to head across the strait. The two white-robed monks stopped skipping rocks. Long Sword left his place on the high rock. Blue Rice took another swig of saké. Everyone headed for the boat.

Mochizuki seemed as ready as he would ever be, having munched what hay he wanted, leaving most of the bale scattered among the rocks. She led her mount onto the planks and down the wooden walkway, out of the cliff's shadow and into the brilliant sunlight. She then paused and took in a deep breath of salt air. She raised the paper with the poem she had translated the night before—less a poem, more a prayer.

She softly whispered:

A winding overgrown trail
Leading down from soaring peaks
Ageless trees at the Barrier Strait
Blue skies merge with churning waters

She had scarcely finished its parsimonious syllables when she realized her whispers were loud enough to be overheard by Long Sword, for he studied her with more than mild interest.

Now, as their eyes finally met, she took him in with but a glance: older, balding—though she could not be sure of that for he wore a braided, black-lacquered *amigasa* shade-hat that half-hid his face. In spite of the hat, she saw that he was clean shaven, which likely meant that he wished not to call attention to the fact he had started to turn gray. Yet the creases that had crept into his face revealed he was at least twice her age, maybe a little bit more.

He looked as if he was about to speak to her when the senchou called for everyone to board. At this Long Sword sat down and removed his amigasa. *Bald, indeed.* He then continued, piece by piece, to remove his armor—lacquered indigo *kozane* platelets interlaced with dark orange silk cords.

"First crossing, samurai-*kun*?" he muttered in her direction, though not exactly politely, for he had addressed her as *kun*, in the way an older man might address a younger one.

She shook her head.

"Humph," he snorted. "If we end up going in, you can't swim in *that*." He jabbed his thumb at her, indicating her heavy battle gear.

"If it comes to that, I'll let my horse do the work," she remarked grimly. "I'll just hold onto my mount. He'll do all the swimming for me."

"Horse, eh?" He frowned, fussing with his armor fastenings. "Fancy. Fancy Taka boy. Did your father give you that horse for your genpuku?"

Genpuku? Boy? He thinks I am twelve. Doesn't he notice I am taller than he? Well . . . it's not that I want him to know who I really am.

The senchou walked up to her, gesturing to the boarding planks, and softly said, "Your mount, Taka-sama. You can board now."

She led Mochizuki forward. Despite the colt's whinnies of protest, Yamabuki, with the help of the senchou, who showed his experience with battle horses, maneuvered her spirited mount across the planks and onto the boat. The senchou helped her lead the colt to the blind, which would shield Mochizuki's ears from the wind and his eyes from the crested rollers of the open waters.

Moments after, Long Sword, last of the travelers to board, sat down, and the crew cast off. As the craft drifted into the current, the boatmen started going through the formalities with ropes and knots known only to sailors. The kobune floated out of the shelter afforded by the bluffs and into a stiff breeze. The senchou's two helpers smartly hoisted a faded patchwork sail that quickly filled with wind, lending purpose to the boat's motion, carrying it straight into the main channel.

Eleven

No Reason to Conceal Herself

"SMOOTH TODAY," ONE OF the crew called out to no one in particular. "The sea deity seems satisfied."

The morning haze continued to lift and the features of the Great Isle became sharper. Quiet conversations started up among the passengers, all except for Long Sword, who surreptitiously studied her from his seat at the stern, next to his stacked weapons and armor, just ahead of the senchou at the tiller.

What's he interested in? The dispatches? Doubtful. Still . . .

She decided, for the moment at least, to give Long Sword no further thought.

Blue Rice worked his way to the middle of the boat and sat across from Yamabuki, his hands folded in his lap.

"Are those forts?" he asked, lifting one hand to point at mounds on hillsides and hilltops along the shore of the Isle of Unknown Fires behind them and the shore of the Main Isle ahead of them.

Yamabuki nodded.

Blue Rice took a gulp from his sake bottle. "But there have been no invasions in centuries. We are at peace."

"Rulers can change overnight," Yamabuki said. "'Peace with one, then war with his son,' or so the adage goes." She paused. "And there are always pirates."

"Pirates?" He looked up and down the channel.

Yamabuki smiled wryly. "A few cutthroats in most cases, with whom we'd deal straightaway. Heian-kyō is too far away to grant us *tsuibu kampu* in time."

"A Warrant of Pursuit?" Blue Rice seemed to be quite ignorant of how troops were mustered.

"We can legally act without consulting Heian-kyō," she said with some pride, "because if raiders come, we have to respond immediately. Our city of Dazaifu is almost an auxiliary capital. We trade with the world. It's why our isle has more wealth, goods, knowledge, and learning than anywhere in the empire. You noticed Mochizuki. Where do you think we could get such a fine steed?"

Long Sword exhaled loudly, apparently listening to her conversation. She continued to ignore him and pointed west, out across the sea to the horizon. Blue Rice glanced at the expanse and took another swig from his flask.

"But the Nagato District," she said with a flick of her hand to indicate the other side of the channel, "that's another matter. Many call it by its literal name, 'Main Gate.' The Ōe clan are the stopper on the bottle, the bottle being the rest of the empire. Their forts also stand at the ready." She thought about what she'd just said, and added, "We certainly will be interrogated by the *sakimori* barrier guards."

Blue Rice cast a worried look at Nagato.

She grinned and shook her head. "You don't look or act much like a pirate. I do not think they will bother with you."

He gave a small grin in return, took another swig, and lay back down in the bottom of the boat.

She, on the other hand, rose to her feet. Her previous passages had been on much larger craft—ones which could hold a royal carriage, its oxen, and sixty mounted samurai. Those crossings took most of an hour. On the royal journeys, it was required that a noblewoman, young as she was then, remain out of plain sight and away from the punishing sun, which in turn meant that she as of yet had never enjoyed a clear mid-channel view of the strait, the isles, or the Leeward Sea. But today in the open craft, with no reason to conceal herself, for the first time she got an unobstructed glimpse of the Isle of Unknown Fires from out in the strait. Her home isle's snowcapped inland mountaintops shone brightly.

Already six day's journey from the outer edge of Great Bay Province, she strained to see any smoke from Shinmoe-dake, but found no sign of the volcanic plume. *A long way from home*, she thought to herself.

The sail fluttered and flapped against the penetrating blue sky. And though the breeze was strong, moist, and cool, she remained warm, comfortable, and dry in her armor. Arms akimbo, she let the air sweep over her, her hakama fluttering, tugged by the wind, just like the sail. Perhaps it was her imagination, but the small, low-slung kobune seemed to move faster than the larger ships of previous crossings.

Her interest flowed to the other passengers, whose conversation she could not help but overhear. From what she could gather, the two genial monks, who were about her age or slightly older, were embarked on a pilgrimage to an important temple near the summit of a sacred mountain. The fretful merchant and his apprentices were on their way north, possibly as far as the Heavenly Capital, where it was rumored that fabrics fetched higher prices. The boatmen talked among themselves, mostly focusing on keeping the kobune steered toward the spot on the opposite shore, where more passengers undoubtedly waited for the return trip. Blue Rice lay in the bottom of the boat with his cap across his face, seemingly half-asleep.

Maybe it was because they were closer to Yamabuki's age, or they still had the visual acuity of youth, but she was taken slightly by surprise when one of the monks said in a loud whisper to her, "A Taka warrior—and a *woman*, at that!"

Twelve

Are My Teeth Black?

The monk's name was Akibō—"bō" being the suffix that monks added to their names to denote their religious status. The other monk was called Iebō. She knew monks were discouraged from discoursing with females, but these two seemed at ease with her—as if she were a sister. Yamabuki had a momentary fantasy where she, like them, had become an itinerant Buddhist. Then her name would have been Yamabukiama—Yamabuki the nun.

"Have you been to the Main Isle before?" asked Iebō.

"It's been some years," she said.

"But that was before you were a samurai." Akibō nodded in answer to his own question.

"Heian-kyō is a magnificent city," said Iebō.

"That it is," she said.

"With palaces and wonders. And more people than you'd ever thought existed," Iebō said. "Tens of thousands of people."

"Hundreds of thousands," she corrected.

Akibō cocked his head, casting quick glances at both Blue Rice and Long Sword. "You seem to be traveling by yourself."

"No." Yamabuki grinned slightly. "I have my colt."

Iebō's eyes sparkled as he laughed. "True. A good companion. Those born under the sign of the horse are said to be quick and smart, though sometimes so quick and so smart that people will say that such a person is hotheaded."

Yamabuki laughed along with him. "Then you know Mochizuki well. He is all of that."

"Do you know the places to stay on your way to Heian-kyō?" Iebō asked.

Yamabuki grinned enigmatically.

Akibō said in a friendly tone, "We know many temples along the imperial highway at which to stay, friendly to monk and warrior alike."

She began to wonder why these monks were seemingly asking her to accompany them, when suddenly she felt the boat slightly list.

In an instant, Long Sword, still at the stern of the craft, was standing. "You!" he shouted almost in accusation, and again addressed her as a familiar. "A woman?"

The boat continued listing slightly as Long Sword made his way forward.

She noticed immediately that his field sword, along with the rest of his blades, lay next to his stacked armor. If he wanted to start trouble, he would not be using those weapons, at least not without retreating to get them.

He scowled, stopping three steps away and pointedly looked her over as if for the first time.

She returned a look of dead calm.

His scowl changed into an expression which on any other face would have been haughty, but on his was more of a grimace. "Are the Taka men so short of warriors that they are training up women as samurai?"

"Are the Ōuchi women not taught how to defend their castles when their husbands are away in battle? Does the blood of the warrior Goddess Jingū no longer flow as strongly as it once did through their veins?"

She knew she should not have made the sly reference to the clan's diluted ancestry, especially since it was not true, but his cheek needed to be checked.

"Do *you* have a husband whose castle *you* defend?" he demanded, eyes narrowed.

"Are my teeth black?" she quipped, and to prove her point she smiled broadly, though not warmly, showing her perfect white teeth. Like all unmarried upper class women, she did not blacken her teeth in the practice of *haguro*.

He begrudgingly snorted a laugh. "Women who walk around with swords should not go around reciting poetry."

"But women who can use them can," she said without making it sound like a challenge.

"Better to keep your mouth shut and your eyes open." He glared at her.

Blue Rice stirred, looking sleepily toward Long Sword. "We both heard the Taka warrior's poem. If someone were to judge her fighting skill based on her poetry, they would be very wise not to contest with her."

By now, everyone had fallen silent. The only sound was the lapping rush of waters, the cry of gulls, and the flapping of the sail.

"So." Long Sword quieted down, realizing that most everyone

else aboard, even a crewmember, had withdrawn forward, away from him—which was not all that far given the size of the boat. As for the senchou, he stayed at his station, seemingly indifferent to the warriors' conversation. For his part, Blue Rice was back to snoring without moving.

"What do the Taka teach their women warriors?" Long Sword's voice was low, almost conversational, though not quite, and this meant he had only changed tactics; whatever his goal in addressing her, she did not know.

Yamabuki stood still, mirroring his outward pretense of calm. "We learn from our teachers. Same as you. Same as everyone."

"Teachers . . . ha!" He directed some latent ire toward some unnamed teachers. "There's fencing-hall teaching and then there's real-world experience. There're things they can't teach in some training hall . . . things you only know by living and fighting and killing—and you don't get that from some old fool."

He took a step forward. Her pulse quickened. She remained relaxed, ready, saying nothing.

"Like back on shore. You didn't remove your armor like I did. If this boat were to capsize, you'd have to swim for it—and don't look to that fancy horse of yours to save you, either—he won't. If you were my pupil, you wouldn't get away with that."

His pupil? My!

There was what seemed like a long silence before he sniffed, "Ever been in a duel?"

She smiled.

Akibō and Iebō cast uneasy sideways glances at each other.

Thirteen

We Shall Fight With Sticks

"Ever kill a man? That takes cold blood." The samurai looked at her, his eyes searching hers, then nodded to himself, "I can see you haven't . . . but I have . . . plenty of times. I fought in the Hōgen Rebellion—for the *victorious* side!—and it's nothing like those old fools tell you."

Yamabuki inclined her head politely, indicating that she had heard his words.

Why was this warrior saying all this? She knew that if she waited, she would find out, so she sat down and let him continue. What else could she do?

And indeed, he continued:

"It's nothing like they have you stage in some *dojo*. It's not like that. Everyone's cutting at each other. Blood everywhere. Limbs hacked away. Screams. Oh, the screams. Screams like nothing you've ever heard. Anger. Pain. Fear. Despair. They cry for Buddha's help, but Buddha doesn't help. Better to cry for a quick death and hope your enemy listens, because in battle they'll *beg* you to finish them off. Blood. Lots of blood. More than you've ever seen, girl."

Yamabuki's mouth twisted. "A woman isn't afraid of blood. She sees it every month of her life."

Long Sword snorted, his expression sour. "A girl with a tongue as sharp as her sword. Duels are different. They're more like the fencing hall. Ever practiced with real steel against someone who's not obliged to hold back?"

"The Ōuchi train that way with each other?"

At the mention of the Ōuchi, Long Sword once again darkened, and she began to suspect that he had had a falling-out with the clan. *Why else would he be traveling by himself, in the opposite direction?* she considered, reflecting upon the forty Ōuchi warriors who had just returned to the Isle of Unknown Fires. *Perhaps he's an outcast who no longer serves a clan. A* ronin, *a person of the wave. Maybe that is why he acts this way.*

Long Sword continued. "We use dull blades. Can't really get too hurt. It's very different from wooden swords." He paused for a moment. "In fact I have a proposal. When we reach shore, we shall fight each other with sword-length sticks, just like you're probably used to in your dojo. If you win, you go on your way. If I win, you become my student and learn the *real* art of war from someone who has experienced it firsthand."

"You are very kind," she answered politely, "but I am duty-bound to reach my final destination and I cannot tarry."

"Where are you headed?" He grew dark again.

She shrugged, for where she was going, or why, was not something to be shared with anyone, least of all him.

"Heian-kyō," he said flatly. "You are headed for capital, *ne*?"

She still did not answer him.

The seas grew choppy and the boat started to sway. "Prepare!"

yelled the senchou, and indeed the boat turned, heading directly on the final leg toward the landing on the Main Isle. "Weather coming in," the senchou called out.

Long Sword gave Yamabuki a look, turned, and made his way back toward his gear as the boat started to jostle.

Muted cheers erupted from the people at the shore—in both greeting and delight that the boat would be there in time to make a crossing back today.

As the crew dropped sail, a temple bell tolled out the last quarter of the Hour of the Snake. The entire seagoing leg had taken but half an hour.

Blue Rice sat up. If it was possible for a man to have a completely green complexion, he had achieved it; at least that is what Yamabuki thought. His saké bottle, sans stopper, lay in the corner of the deck.

"The last bit was rough," she said.

Blue Rice appeared to grow more ill at the mere mention of the rough seas. He gasped and pointed over the side.

"A water fox!"

Yamabuki's eyes shot to the place he pointed. Nothing. She shook her head.

He pointed, shaking his finger at the spot. "Red! Fox face. Fox tail. Laughing."

She wondered if his saké had gotten the better of him. She had not only heard of, but also seen, people who were so possessed by drink, or lack of it at the moment, that they saw what wasn't there or, rather, did not understand the things they did see.

"Ah," Yamabuki's eyes narrowed. "Maybe a sea lion. They can look a bit like foxes."

Blue Rice snapped, "I know what a sea lion looks like! I am not some fool." He rose to his feet. "I once was of a daimyō lineage," he thundered, "and *that* was not a sea lion."

Fourteen

What Lord Do You Serve?

The senchou guided the boat toward the dock and the shore crew pulled it in.

Yamabuki immediately headed forward to her colt. While the fabric merchant and his five helpers scuttled about, she moved Mochizuki toward the gangplank, determined to be off the boat before the cart got in the way. Again with the help of the senchou, she led her mount onto shore.

The horse was not pleased with the crowd. He snorted, threatening to rear as she led him through the waiting passengers. The commoners quickly parted at the sight of the prancing hooves.

She took a quick look at the stern of the craft—Long Sword, along with his armor, was thankfully gone.

What a strange man.

She turned to find Akibō and Iebō waiting for her. They bowed and gave her a small unrequested blessing. Iebō said, "Maybe you should travel with us."

"Hai!" Akibō agreed.

Iebō added, "That Ōuchi warrior's looking for trouble."

Yamabuki inhaled. “As much as I appreciate your kindness, I believe I am not in danger.” *And I doubt I’ll need the help of two unarmed monks.*

The monks shifted uncomfortably and bowed to her.

She bowed in return. “You go on ahead. Have a safe journey to your temple.”

They turned and somewhat stiffly headed toward the inland road.

There was no need for wooden planking since this beach, unlike the one below Kita, was not nearly as rocky. The soil was quite sandy. *Muddy. It rained harder here last night than back across the channel.* Getting Mochizuki to the road would be much easier along these low bank shores. *No cliff to climb*, she smiled to herself.

She looked along the coast, a series of coves. The beach close to the kobune was backed up with carts and goods, too many to fit all aboard for the upcoming departure.

No wonder the senchou was so quick to leave Kita. He knew he had a throng awaiting. They had probably been forced to give up their places to the Ōuchi warriors who had crossed earlier.

Meanwhile, the fabric merchants, who finally got their cart off the kobune, now struggled to get its wheels through the sand.

Yamabuki looked above the high-water mark, where about ten Ōe sakimori blocked the path. They were dressed in black warrior-tunics, each displaying the bright orange-on-white Ōe clan emblem: a single upright arrow feather.

The guards struck her as overly grim for merely checking people headed inland.

A man wearing a gold medallion, the symbol of a leader, stood at their center. Two of his lieutenants flanked him, one on each side.

All three carried bows, arrows, and long swords. The remaining guards carried only polearms. None of the Ōe wore battle armor.

As she approached them, they were already busily questioning Akibō and Iebō, who held out their alms bowls. The guards promptly responded by sending them packing, empty handed.

The sakimori then eyed Yamabuki and her mount. One of the lieutenants, not much older than she, looked her up and down, and not in the way one warrior might look at another, nor in the way a man might look at a woman that he found interesting. It was as if he were searching for some flaw in her armor in which he could find weakness or fault.

"Who are you and what Lord do you serve?" he asked, affecting a tough manner.

"I am Yamabuki of the Taka and I serve that clan," she said simply.

"Where are you headed?" he asked.

"Heian-kyō."

"On what business?"

"In the service of Lord Moroto."

The Ōe men flashed looks to one other.

"Beautiful mount, Taka-san," said the leader as he let his eyes sweep over Mochizuki. "Young."

"Barely more than a yearling," she said, bowing slightly in acknowledgment.

"How long have you had him?" he asked.

"I raised him from a foal."

"Great Bay District has *fine* horses."

The other lieutenant, the plain looking one, began to speak, "There is a fee for those who—"

The leader raised his hand and the lieutenant stopped mid-sentence, stunned but obedient. The man in charge waved her on. "Have a safe journey, Taka-san."

They had barely exchanged small bows of departure when she heard a sudden commotion.

The guards, as one, looked at the shore behind her. As she turned, she saw Blue Rice in the distance, his hands over his mouth, running headlong across the beach toward a clump of bushes and trees above the shoreline.

He's going to lose his stomach.

"Halt!" yelled one of the guards. "Ha!" other guards echoed.

Either Blue Rice did not hear the sakimori yelling at him, or he was too embarrassed to care. Now starting to double over in the throes of nausea, he raised one arm, waving at the shouting men, indicating that they should wait.

Obviously his saké cure has failed, Yamabuki thought to herself, shaking her head.

Yamabuki started to say, "He's just seasick—"

But before she could finish her sentence, the tough lieutenant had already drawn his bow and shot an arrow.

Yamabuki gasped.

The arrow lodged in Blue Rice's ribcage. He stumbled and fell, losing his stomach. At first he vomited what looked like what he had eaten, mostly saké, but then blood. He managed to stand up, his eyes in pain, throwing his arms open as if asking, "Why?"

People in the waiting crowd screamed.

Yamabuki choked.

Another arrow hit Blue Rice, this time in the chest. He looked upward, grabbed the arrow shaft, staggered, then fell back.

"Right in the heart," smirked one of the guards.

"Perfect shot, Misaki-san," another said with admiration.

For a moment, Yamabuki wanted to run over to Blue Rice. She wanted to say something. Do something. But nothing could be said. Nothing could be done.

Her mouth twisted, she looked at the man in charge, her palms open, questioning.

He pursed his lips, shrugged slightly, and whispered, "He shouldn't have run."

FIFTEEN

WHO WILL SAY THE SUTRAS?

YAMABUKI LED MOCHIZUKI UP a road that sloped gradually and gently inland.

At the first bend that was out of the sight of the beach, she paused by a dry fallen log that rested on sandy soil near trees where cherry buds bloomed. Tethering Mochizuki, she sat on the log and only then realized that she was shaking—not in fear, but in anger.

Why am I upset?

It was a local matter. She did not know Blue Rice. She had not met him until this morning. They had not exchanged all that many words. She didn't even know his name or where he was from. Why would she feel this way? But then she knew. It was the look on his face. His dismay. The shock. He had done nothing more than lose his stomach. Hadn't the guards seen that countless times?

Who would now bury him? Who would take a lock of his hair back to his home village? Who would say the sutras to rest his young soul after having died on a strange and foreign beach?

She gathered some small stones, stacking a simple mound

behind the shelter of the log. She stood up to cut several cherry sprigs with her *tantō*-style dagger. She walked over to Mochizuki, reached into her saddle pouch, where she found three incense sticks and her bamboo canteen. She placed the flowers around the stone mound and spread the sand to hold the incense sticks, which she then lit, placing them around the tiny cenotaph. She pushed three copper coins into the sand. Commoners placed coins in various orifices of the corpse—mouth, ears, eyes, anus—to help the dead journey into whatever lay beyond life. Today the sand would have to suffice. Finally, she unstoppered her flask to carefully pour a good helping of her saké around the marker's perimeter.

"Forgive me, Blue Rice, for I am no priest. I hope this *Omiki* will do and that the Gods will be pleased." Softly she chanted Shintō remembrances to honor the dead.

She bowed low, turned, packed up, then took Mochizuki's reins and returned to the main road.

Three hours of daylight remained.

Sixteen

It's a Long Road, Lady Taka

NAKAGAWA HAD ADVISED HER that since the southern coasts of the Main Isle at this point consisted of rocky bluffs, the road through the mountains was the fastest and easiest way to Heian-kyō.

She rode along the level road until she came to Akamagaseki, a small settlement of about fifty buildings located just at the point where the main north-south road steepened.

There she found sweet water to replenish her canteen and bought a handful of warm rice from a street vendor, but she did not have time for more than that. Within a day, two at most, she would face the passes that, this early in the spring, might still hold snow.

As she left Akamagaseki, the road sloped up sharply. She looked back over her shoulder from the higher vantage. The morning sun rose over fishing villages and farms on the fertile coastal plain below. In the far distance, she could barely make out the kobune, mid-channel, making its way back to Kita.

Back at the beach, the six fabric merchants and their fabric-laden cart were only just starting to make their way toward the town.

Now she walked, leading Mochizuki along the highway, up into the hills. The fragrance of cherry trees in full flower replaced the scent of the sea. The chirping of crickets, a sign of good luck, filled the forests. The far-away bell of Akamagaseki temple began to sound out the hour. A woodcock joined in. Then the cry of a black kite.

She paused to count the number of bells. "Nine strikes. Hear that? The sun is directly overhead. The Hour of the Horse, Mochizuki. Your hour."

The day, which up until then had been growing progressively warmer, now grew cool as a squall blew in from what had been a cloudless sky. A steady rain began to fall.

She walked along the Main Isle road for some time, protected from the worst of the weather by the leafing tree branches that arched over the road, until she came to a clearing where someone had erected a very small Shintō shrine. It was typical of so many such shrines along the highway. What was not typical was the Buddhist monk standing before it, his back to her, seemingly praying to the Old Gods.

Either seeing or sensing her approach, he turned around. He had a bottle of saké in his hand. He looked at her and took a generous swig.

"Iebō?" she said in puzzlement.

Though he grinned, his expression had lost all boyish charm. His eyes narrowed like a snake's. His white flowing robes were tied back in the way warriors secured their sleeves before a duel.

"How is it that you are here?" she asked politely.

"I paused here to pray."

"A Buddhist praying at a Shintō shrine?"

"Does it matter?" Iebō seemed dismissive.

"Where is Akibō?"

"Behind you."

She turned her head. No more than ten paces away, Akibō stood in the middle of the road, his sleeves also tied back in dueling style.

Yamabuki revealed no emotion.

Mochizuki snorted, agitated, as Akibō slowly moved toward Yamabuki.

"What are you after?"

"After? Nothing." Iebō smiled.

"Nothing?"

"It's a long road, Lady Taka," Akibō said at last.

"*Lady* Taka? How is it that you call me by that title?" Yamabuki's sword hand slowly slid to Tiger Claw's hilt.

Seventeen

To Win, You Have to Kill Us Both

Iebō sniffed. "You say too much Aki."

"Aki, is it? Not Aki-*bō*?" she sneered. "Your monk's vows could not survive even the crossing of The Barrier." She glared. "But then again, you were never monks to begin with, were you? And *you*, your name isn't Iebō either, is it?"

His mouth grew ugly. "Does that surprise you?"

"Who do you work for?"

"Let's say we hold gold higher than Gods." Iebō lips twisted petulantly. "Someone wants the two dispatches you carry."

"Two dispatches?" Yamabuki's tone remained flat.

"Don't toy with us!" Aki sneered.

With that, Iebō, or whatever he called himself, tugged on his walking staff.

In one motion, he pulled the top off, revealing what was actually a ninja-style long sword that had been sheathed within the staff.

"You two fools think you can win," she said in a low voice, not about to show fear. "Give this up. Run for your lives while you still can. There may be two of you, but I warn you, I am well trained and I'm wearing full *yoroi* armor."

"Maybe so," Iebō' said, his mouth drawn into a line, "but it will take no more than a nick to end you."

Then she noticed a honey-like substance that glistened at the tip of Iebō's blade.

He answered her unvoiced question. "The walking sticks are hollow, but not empty. They hold something *special.*" He thumped the butt of the walking staff against the ground.

"Once your skin is broken, even if only slightly, you'll be paralyzed. Your death will be almost immediate, so you might even wish to thank us. It'll be over for you quickly."

With that Aki drew his blade, which was no different from Iebō's, gleaming with the thick contagion on its tip.

She again vividly pictured the final moments of her father's bodyguard, Giichi. Did Iebō and Aki use the same poison? *Possibly. Abundant here at the strait. A local delicacy.*

Yamabuki's mouth drew into a thin line. "How do I know that it's poison at all?"

"Why don't we find out on your horse?" Iebō sneered as he stepped toward Mochizuki.

She tore Tiger Claw from its scabbard and stepped in to guard the colt; but this, alas, put her between the assailants. Confidently, they circled like wild dogs closing in for the kill.

Her mouth went dry. She knew that it would take more than a glancing blow for anyone to get the better of her armor, but the armor was not immune to every type of attack. Yoroi was meant to blunt killing blows, or strikes that maimed—those delivered to the head, torso, arms, and wrists—not incidental scratches.

And by how the two assassins handled themselves, she suspected they knew where armor was vulnerable, where they might deliver the poison most easily.

The two false monks looked at each other, exchanged a signal, and pounced as one.

Aki rushed her, feinting, his poison-tipped blade lashing out. Yamabuki blocked, knocking the ninja sword aside. No sooner had she parried Aki than Iebō drove his blade toward her. His sword tip, like a ridged viper with dripping venom, almost cut her leg. Yamabuki blocked him in time, only to have Aki move in from the other side to deliver yet another thrust.

The sword's grim tip flashed in front of her eyes, narrowly missing her face.

"You can't win!" Aki shouted.

"Ha!" Yamabuki spat.

"To win, you have to kill us both. All we need do is cut you, and only once," Aki sneered.

"Bad odds," Iebō laughed.

Aki and Iebō attacked simultaneously. She turned her sword, defending, blocking, and reversing against each of them. The two assassins repeated this ploy over and over.

As sweat trickled down Yamabuki's reddening face, Iebō called out, "I can see the girl's getting tired. Weak. Exhausted."

"We're getting more rest than she is," Aki snorted. "And she's getting hot inside that armor." He suddenly made a thrust. She deflected and lashed out with a spirited strike that grazed his shoulder.

He laughed, seemingly unaffected. "Too bad you don't have the venom on *your* blade, or it might have done some good."

"I have venom," she shouted, "in my heart." She sprang forward, armor and all, driving her sword toward Aki's heart. He was agile and leapt back.

Yet he was more exhausted than he let on, and she managed to pierce him just below his collarbone. All at once the white robe at his shoulder blossomed bright red.

Staggering backward, he tried to make it appear that he was hardly hurt, but almost immediately he collapsed into a squatting position.

"That won't kill me," he snarled, but then coughed and started to bleed from the corner of his mouth.

"Maybe," she gasped. "Maybe I'll just wait for you to bleed out."

Iebō snarled and moved toward Yamabuki.

She backed up.

Aki barked, "What are you waiting for?"

With force enough to pierce her armor, Iebō thrust his blade.

Yamabuki leapt backward. Iebō missed. Yamabuki delivered a counter, which he eluded.

Aki, now crawling on the ground, moaned, "She getting tired! She's spent! Do it!"

Yamabuki backed toward a stand of trees at the clearing's edge.

Aki gasped as his robe grew evermore sopped in blood.

Iebō pursued nimbly. Laughing wickedly. Taunting. He raised his blade to remind her of the dark liquid on its tip.

Without warning, something cut her left cheek. Blood spurted.

But Iebō was still more than a sword length away. Aki still remained slumped by the roadside.

Who? How?

Aki gave a weak laugh. "I got you!" He coughed up more gore.

Her eyes darted down. Her blood was on a jagged rock that lay at her feet. Obviously, despite his wound, Aki had managed to throw the rock and hit her. But had he dipped it in poison?

She waited. The short moment seemed to take forever.

Iebō must have wondered as well, for he stood still, waiting for Yamabuki to collapse.

She breathed. Just pain. No poison.

Just a rock.

She glanced back at Aki. Having crawled as far as he could, he lay face down in the dirt, not moving. A red trail wet the soil.

Iebō muttered, "Now you die."

Eighteen

I've Never lost a Duel

"Only two of us now, ninja," she said through gritted teeth. "Let's see how good you are with your blade."

Iebō moved toward her. "Just a scratch. It's all I need to deliver. Then you're dead."

"Like Aki?" she sneered.

Iebō flicked his blade, sending poison in her direction. She dodged just in time as a splotch of venom flew right by her face, very close to the open cut on her cheek.

"Keep doing that and there won't be enough of your little concoction left to kill an ant."

They were both exhausted. Blades extended, they again began moving in a circle, each waiting for the other to make a mistake.

Iebō snarled, "I've never lost a duel."

"I suppose Aki hadn't either," she hissed, "and he was more skilled with the blade than you. That I can easily see."

Iebō attacked. Sword flashing, he screamed, "Die!"

She parried. This time she countered vigorously. One. Two. Three strikes. She moved in on him all at once.

Iebō barely managed to defend, quickly backing up.

There was movement behind Iebō. Had Aki rallied? Yamabuki caught colors. Indigo and dark orange.

There was a guttural shout. A field sword sliced down, seemingly from nowhere, cutting Iebō from his right collar bone on down through the left side of his rib cage. Blood sprayed everywhere. His upper torso, head and all, simply sloughed away to the ground, landing with a thud.

Long Sword!

Before the rest of Iebō's body had fully fallen to the ground, Long Sword stomped off toward Aki and drove the nodachi through Aki's back, through the heart. If he was not dead before, he was surely dead now.

"Cowards!" Long Sword thundered.

Yamabuki fought to catch her breath. She reached into her sash-sleeve to remove a piece of paper with which to dab the blood from her face. She then wiped her blade, careful not to touch any poison that it might have picked up while clashing with Aki's and Iebō's ninja swords.

In the meantime, Long Sword pulled papers from his jacket sleeve to wipe the blood from his blade.

When they finished, Long Sword and Yamabuki let go of the papers and the slight breeze carried the bloody tissues into the trees. The two mutually sheathed their weapons.

"Why?" asked Yamabuki, still catching her breath.

"I knew they were ninja. Cowards disguised as holy men, using fugu venom!"

"You knew?" she repeated.

"You're *so* naïve."

"Naïve!" Yamabuki's eyes flashed.

"Humph," he snorted. "I told you on the boat to keep your eyes open, but you didn't keep your eyes open at all. It was obvious. I saw it back on the beach at Kita. They were dressed as Tendai sect, but they did not behave like Buddhist monks. I watched them eating oysters. They cut and shucked them with their own knives. That's outright killing from the Tendai way of looking at things."

He grunted. "But you're no Buddhist, are you? Shintō, if even that, ne? You're a warrior. Killing some oysters means nothing to you, does it? Doesn't to me, either. Nor to them."

Long Sword shrugged, dismissively throwing his hand in the direction of the two corpses.

"And the way they spoke."

He continued in a speech that mocked theirs, deliberately aping a failed attempt at the upper class manner, adding feminine softeners, effetely rolling his eyes skyward:

"'We know *many* temples along the imperial highway at which to stay; *friendly* to *monk* and *warrior* alike.' Ha!"

He laughed. "That a monk would *dare* approach a warrior and *dare* speak with such familiarity! Oh, girl, you have so much yet to learn."

He looked her up and down.

"At first I thought you might even be working with them and that I was the target. I suspected that when you stopped for 'Gankyū' before the crossing, back up on Foot Trail."

"Stopped for *Eyeball*?" Yamabuki looked askance. "Who is Eyeball?"

NINETEEN

A DECISION YOU WON'T LIVE TO REGRET

"I JUST SAID: GANKYŪ. HE'LL do anything for any official, for a price. He's no crabber. Never trust someone who doesn't drink saké. They're hiding something about themselves for which they are ashamed. When I saw the two of you together, I figured either you were working with him, or you were easily taken in. Obviously it was the latter."

"So he works for the Ōuchi?"

He paused to contemplate her again. "No. He won't work for any clan, but he'll work for traitors within one." He raised his eyebrow. "Taka traitors."

A look of ire crossed Yamabuki's face.

Long Sword rubbed his chin. "I overheard them say something about some dispatches you're carrying."

Yamabuki did not react.

"Don't try and fool me. I heard those two say that's what they wanted."

Her eyes narrowed.

"Ah!" he growled. "I don't care about your foolish scrolls. You can wipe the *kuso* off your ass with each and every one of them as far as I am concerned, but did it ever occur to you that you were sent out alone and yet somehow someone knew that you carried dispatches? Why not just send a detachment if these scrolls are all so important? I'll wager you don't even know what's on them, or did you dare read them?"

He took a long look at her. "No. You didn't." He sighed. "For all you know, you're carrying blank documents, or forgeries that are *supposed* to fall into someone else's hands. It's obvious that you were sent out as bait to smoke someone else out and it looks like it worked, *chibi*," he said, calling her a runt. "And now that they've failed, do you think this will be the last attempt they'll make?" He snorted back a laugh. "It's only the first! It's good that I am trained." He nodded to himself. "Good that I took it on myself to follow you. These are the sorts of things," he sniffed, "that you can't learn in a training hall."

Yamabuki did not have even the slightest look of appreciation on her face. "That you got involved is true," she said, "and that your sword dispatched the one calling himself Iebō is undeniable, but one of them was already down when you entered the fray. He was bleeding from the mouth. I got his lung. He was finished with or without you." She held her voice steady. "I am confident that the other one would have fallen quickly."

"You're just telling yourself a story. I watched the whole thing. I only stepped in when I saw that you were in over your head."

"The only way to have found out was if you had stayed out of it."

Long Sword chuckled. "There's that sharp tongue again." He paused. "Come with me and I'll give you real training, the kind you did not get from the Taka."

Yamabuki said nothing, looking at him impassively.

He snorted. "You're like the Ōuchi. You're afraid to get hurt during training. I ask, 'When are they going to find out their students do not have enough skill?' They'll find out, just as you did just now. You aren't ready. But I shall teach you, and in a few years, if you survive, you'll be on your way, and better for it. Remember our agreement back on the boat? We shall fight with sticks, and if you lose, you will follow me."

Yamabuki quietly stepped toward Mochizuki, taking his bridle. "I shall be on my way. I am a Taka *bushi* on an assignment, regardless of your speculations about intrigue, and I have made no agreement with you, so if you would, please stand out of the road so that I may pass."

"If not more ninja, there are rough men out there—and not kind like me. They'll have their way with you, you know."

So that's *why he keeps gawking at me. He wants to have* nan'in *with me! It's what he's wanted all along. First when he thought I was a boy, and now that he knows I'm a woman.*

"I am able to take care of myself," she said firmly.

"I've seen what you can do. You didn't do so well. You owe me your life."

"As I just said, you do not know how that match would have ended. You interfered. I owe you nothing."

He grew grim. "Be careful, girl. Careful before you make a decision that you won't live to regret."

"I will be on my way." She glared at him.

"You won't last!" He glared back. "You'll be a morsel for the first truly tough guy who comes along."

"We shall find out."

"We find out now!" His steel hissed against his scabbard. He raised the field sword over his head in the prepare position—an excellent position where the reach of the blade was at its optimum. He stood, supreme in his indigo yoroi, with the look of a man who expected only victory or capitulation.

"You've drawn steel against me," she said, dropping her voice low, "so tell me, please, what is your name, so that I know who it is that I am about to kill."

Twenty

There Will Be No Second Chance

"So you would dare to challenge me!" Long Sword's cheeks flushed, for Yamabuki had taken the next step in a formal duel: the request for an exchange of names. In a tone certainly lower than hers, he obliged her, growling, "I am Shima Sa-me. It means 'Shark Island.' I've killed too many to count. Easily more than that boatload of Ōuchi earlier today . . . and now I'll add a girl to my list. We'll soon see what those old fools have taught you, sorry though you'll be for it."

"I am Taka Tori Yamabuki, daughter of General Moroto, who is also my teacher, and no fool."

"Moroto's daughter, eh?" He lifted his chin in disdain. "Well, it can't be helped." He paused again, then commanded at last, "You want to fight? Then draw!"

She did not. Instead she commanded, "Out of my way!" Again resorting to the lowest register she could muster, she growled, "I must pass." She led her mount forward, her left hand on Tiger Claw's hilt.

"What if I just add a nick to your *other* cheek?"

The noon sun glinted off his blade. The nodachi's reach was breathtaking. He moved toward her.

Yamabuki let go of Mochizuki's reins and backed up slowly, not taking her eyes off Shima's. His eyes, not his blade, would show when he would strike.

"You afraid? Afraid to draw, chibi?"

She recalled Nakagawa's words, "*A field sword is designed to bring down horses as they run past. It's meant to do battle in the wide open.*"

She certainly was not some foolish horse about to gallop past him in the open. She backed up carefully, retreating toward the trees; but immediately she found her feet were on progressively rougher terrain, covered with underbrush and the protruding branches of fallen trees.

She did not dare look away from Shima's gaze to check what was behind her. Still, with few alternatives, she continued to work her way toward the woods.

Shima easily recognized her tactic and immediately flanked her, keeping her parallel to the tree line.

"You didn't think you could escape into the woods that easy, did you?"

He advanced, forcing her onto even more uncertain ground covered with thin new-growth trees. She knew they were too slender to offer cover or protection, for his field sword could shear them like grass. But he did not strike—at least not yet.

She soon found herself in the midst of a maze of nascent yellow pine, none of whose trunks were any thicker than her wrist. Pieces of dry, fallen bark snapped under her feet. The air filled with the scent of humus. The trees smelled of sap.

"Are you going to draw, or have you accepted your fate?"

"There is still time to call this off," Yamabuki hissed. "Once I draw steel, there's no going back."

She watched his jaw set.

"Don't force me kill you," she said flatly.

Obviously angered by her audacious pronouncement, he showed his upper teeth, almost as if he intended to bite her. Then she saw his eyes narrow.

This is it!

He growled like a bear as his field sword shot straight at her throat in the manner of a lance.

Hindered by the underbrush, she twisted sideways in the nick of time.

The sound of cracking wood filled the air as his sword crashed through the saplings. Splinters flew in every direction; but once his nodachi was within the trees, he could not appreciably change its straight-line path.

He snarled, "That was luck!"

He immediately drove the tip at her again, and again she moved out of the way, letting the surrounding saplings swallow the blade.

Shima gritted his teeth. His eyes flashed. "Let's try this, then!"

He swung the field sword horizontally at chest height, slashing his way toward her. *Whoosh!* The sound of the air moving before the sword was almost a howl. The saplings snapped as the nodachi cut down the young trees.

He growled with each swing, further leveling the shrubs each time.

Sweat trickled down Yamabuki's face. In no way had she averted the duel. If anything, she was merely prolonging it. Nakagawa's words again rang in her head: *"Some fights are inevitable. Best get them over quick."*

The answer to the nodachi was *speed.*

Her mouth dry, she grabbed one thick, long branch at her feet.

I'll have only one *chance.*

Yamabuki, her tachi still in its scabbard, bolted from the devastated saplings, brandishing the tree limb.

There will be no second chance.

Sword held high, Shima raced toward Mochizuki to intercept her. But she was not running toward her mount. Instead, she stopped in the middle of the clearing.

I must get him to commit.

"Ha!" he shouted.

He moved toward her, death the one thought clearly written on his face and burning in his mind. Breathing hard. Face red. Eyes red. Teeth bared.

She stood in the open, raising the tree limb. It was about as thick as her wrist and as tall as she.

"Wooden sword," he spat. "Too late for that, girl. It's steel now!"

Nakagawa said, "Even a wooden sword, if it's long enough, can match one of steel."

So far she had always been just out of range, or had found ways to keep him from making a full strike.

So long as his sword swings go unopposed, he controls the field. Controls everything. Controls me.

She knew that he was counting on one last sweep of his nodachi, out in the open, to finish her.

Their eyes locked as he again raised his sword high.

He lunged, planting his right front foot. With a mighty grunt, he swept his long blade horizontally to cut her in half at the waist.

One chance.

She swung the branch as if it were a field sword of her own. Though the wood did not meet his blade, the unexpected countermove momentarily distracted his concentration. Nevertheless his blade kept coming.

Speed.

As it reached her, she leapt to her back foot.

She gasped as the nodachi tip scraped her corselet. She felt its visceral power push her sideways as it tore straight through her dark-green chest protector. The sound of the blade tip slicing open her armor assaulted her ears. But as she had gambled, the tip failed to penetrate to her skin.

It would have been natural for anyone to withdrawal after such a blow with all its damage, but her training instilled in her one final lesson with the nodachi: stepping away was stepping into death.

One chance.

She leapt forward right behind the arc of his sword's swath and delivered a sharp rap to his wrist with the branch.

Shima grimaced but did not let go of the massive field sword as he completed the arc from right to left. Then, in one fluid motion he moved in for a return strike, back from left to right.

He had her now.

As he began his second strike, his arms were held high. When he lifted his arms, it also raised his chest armor, exposing the bottom of his ribcage.

Last chance.

She dropped the tree branch and leapt even closer to him, taking a low, elongated stance. Tiger Claw flew from its scabbard, flashing under the noonday sun. Without changing the trajectory of her sword draw, she flipped the tachi's point forward so that its tip was directed at him. Before he could move, she shifted her weight from back to front and with all her might drove the blade into the vulnerable spot below his ribcage.

He grunted, staggered backward, nodachi still in the overhead position, but then his left leg buckled. Blood trickled from his mouth.

"By a girl," he gasped.

Still holding her blade from her crouched position, she pulled hard, withdrawing the tachi from his side.

"So," he gurgled, "you've finally killed. . . ."

His other leg buckled and he fell face-first onto the road and lay very still.

She stood up, the blood singing in her ears. As she had been trained, she wiped her blade clean and sheathed it.

She tore off her helmet. Her hair, soaking wet, fell around her shoulders. The slight breeze passed through her moist tresses, more than cool—cold. She shivered. She moved her hand to the corselet of her once-pristine battle armor and slid her palm across the gash, sensing the roughness and splinters, and the woven rings of steel now exposed underneath. Her hand shook.

Insects buzzed. Here and there the cries of birds drifted through the now-calm air.

The three bodies lay in the clearing, as much a part of the landscape as the trees, brush, and blossoms and no more animated than the rocks.

She walked to her mount. He snorted. She had not quite caught her breath.

Gripping his reins she paused, looking at the stirrup, then let go.

She opened her mouth to say something to Mochizuki, but realized her teeth were chattering. Tears filled her eyes. She buried her face in the crook of her arm and wept and wept.

Glossary and Reference

Characters

Akibō: A monk.

Blue Rice: A traveler to Honshu; aka Aoi Ine.

Chi-ye: Dancer and attendant at Wakatake; thousand blessings *(literal)*.

Gankyū: Eyeball *(literal)*.

General Moroto: Yamabuki's titular father.

Giichi: A Taka retainer to General Moroto.

Iebō: A monk.

Inu: The innkeeper of Wakatake; dog *(literal)*. Member of the Yūkū family.

Ishi-tsuki: Dancer and attendant at Wakatake; stone moon *(literal)*.

Long Sword: An Ōuchi fencing master; aka Shima Sa-Me.

Misaki: Surname of a Nagato sakimori; three blossoms *(literal)*.

Mochizuki: Yamabuki's Horse; full moon *(literal)*.

Nakagawa: Yamabuki's tutor; middle river *(literal)*.

Ryuma: A hatchet man at Wakatake; winged horse *(literal)*.

Shima Sa-Me: Island Shark.

Yamabuki: Yellow rose *(literal)*.

Glossary

Akamagaseki: City in Nagato on Honshu, across the Barrier Strait from Kita.

Akitsushima: Ancient name of Japan; Autumn Creek Land *(literal)*.

amigasa: Braided straw hat.

awaré: Sorrow; in the Japanese concept, the transience of all things.

Barrier Strait: The Kanmon Strait.

buké: Warrior; equivalent to bushi.

buri: Yellowtail, or amberjack.

bushi: Warrior; equivalent to buké.

chibi: Runt; twerp.

Chikuzen Province: Northwestern-most district of the Isle of Unknown Fires, bordered on north by the Kanmon Strait.

Ch'u-mo: Chinese monk and poet of the T'ang Dynasty (fl. 850–900). Yamabuki translates his poem, "Shengkuo Temple."

daimyō: Ruler of hereditary landholdings; often translated as Lord.

Dazaifu : A city of trade and diplomatic relations with foreign countries.

dojo: Studio, often specifically for martial arts study.

dokkoisho: Refrain of a song or poem; pull hard *(literal)*.

fugu: Puffer fish.

Genpei War: Japanese Civil War of 1180–1185; also spelled Gempei.

genpuku: Coming-of-age ceremony for twelve-year-old boys. At this age, a boy was considered an adult.

Great Bay Province/District: Mythical province near present day Miyazaki and Kagoshima. Home of the Taka clan.

haguro: Teeth blackening, a tradition practiced by married women, and some men.

hai: Yes.

hakama: Split trouser-skirt worn over the kimono, commonly worn by the upper classes in this era.

hanabishi: Fire flower; the Ōuchi mon.

hashi: Chopsticks.

Heian-kyō: The capital of Akitsushima; site of present-day Kyoto.

Hō: Ancient name of China.

Hōgen Rebellion: Japanese insurrection in the summer of 1156.

ine: Rice plant.

Isle of Unknown Fires: Ancient name of isle that today is called Kyushu.

Jingū: Warrior Empress, mother of Hachiman, the War God.

kabuto: Warrior helmet.

kago: Palanquin.

Kanmon Strait: Strait between Honshu and Kyushu.

Kita: City at the Barrier Strait, in Chikuzen.

kobune: Water craft, used to ferry passengers and property.

kozane: Iron platelets sewn together to make armor.

kuge: Aristocracy.

kun: An appellation used in the familiar.

kuso: Shit *(colloquial)*.

Leeward Sea: Body of water known today as the Sea of Japan.

Main Isle: Honshu.

mempo: Facial armor worn by samurai in battle.

Mizuka: Significant trading city on the Isle of Unknown Fires, on the road to the Barrier Strait.

mon: Crest or symbol representing a clan.

mouth-sucking: Kissing.

Nagato: Province on the Main Isle, located on the Barrier Strait, across the strait from Kita. Part of modern-day Yamaguchi Prefecture.

nanigashi: Commoners.

nan'in: Sexual intercourse.

ne: No *(colloquial)*.

New Life Month: A spring month also known as *U no hara.*

ninja: Hired agent, often an assassin.

nodachi: Field sword; a very long, heavy battle sword.

Ōe: Clan in Nagato.

omeko: The female sexual parts *(vulgar)*; crab meat *(literal)*.

Omiki: Saké that's offered to the Gods.

Ōuchi: Clan on the Isle of Unknown Fires and Main Isle.

pillow book: A diary.

pole arm: Weapon on a pole.

ronin: Unemployed samurai.

royal carriage: Ox-drawn cart.

sakimori: Historical name for border guards.

sama: Honorific when addressing a superior.

san: Polite salutation, equal to "Mister" or "Miss"; applies to both genders.

senchou: Boat chief.

Shinmoe-dake: Volcanic mountain on the Isle of Unknown Fires.

tachi: Long sword commonly worn by samurai.

tantō: Dagger.

Taka: Yamabuki's clan; hawk *(literal)*.

Tendai sect: A Buddhist sect.

tessen: War fan made out of metal.

Tiger Claw: Name of Yamabuki's tachi.

Tiger Cub: Name of Yamabuki's personal sword.

toi: Foreign; Korean.

tsuibu kampu: Warrant of Pursuit.

Tsukushi: Another ancient name for Kyushu, Yamabuki's home isle.

Wa: Ancient Chinese name for Japan.

Wakatake: An inn in Kita; young bamboo *(literal)*.

Windward Sea: Pacific Ocean.

yoroi: Full armor.

JAPANESE YEARS, SEASONS, AND TIME

SOLAR STEMS

	Romanji	*Kanji*	*Start Date*	*Name*
1	**Risshun**	立春	February 4	Beginning of spring
2	**Usui**	雨水	February 18	Rain water
3	**Keichitsu**	啓蟄	March 5	Awakening of Insects
4	**Shunbun**	春分	March 20	Vernal equinox
5	**Seimei**	清明	April 4	Clear and bright
6	**Kokuu**	穀雨	April 20	Grain rain
7	**Rikka**	立夏	May 5	Beginning of summer
8	**Shōman**	小満	May 21	Grain Fills
9	**Bōshu**	芒種	June 5	Grain in Ear
10	**Geshi**	夏至	June 21	Summer Solstice
11	**Shōsho**	小暑	July 7	Little Heat
12	**Taisho**	大暑	July 23	Great Heat
13	**Risshū**	立秋	August 7	Beginning of Autumn
14	**Shosho**	処暑	August 23	End of Heat
15	**Hakuro**	白露	September 7	Descent of White Dew
16	**Shūbun**	秋分	September 23	Autumnal Equinox
17	**Kanro**	寒露	October 8	Cold Dew
18	**Sōkō**	霜降	October 23	Descent of Frost
19	**Rittō**	立冬	November 7	Beginning of winter
20	**Shōsetsu**	小雪	November 22	Little Snow
21	**Taisetsu**	大雪	December 7	Great Snow
22	**Tōji**	冬至	December 22	Winter Solstice
23	**Shōkan**	小寒	January 5	Little Cold
24	**Daikan**	大寒	January 20	Great Cold

JAPANESE YEARS

Kiūan 1–6 Jan 25, 1145 to Jan 19, 1151
Kiūan 5 has a 13th month observed starting July 18, 1148

Nimbiō 1–3 Jan 20, 1151 to Feb 13, 1154
Nimbiō 1 has a 13th month observed starting May 18, 1151
Nimbiō 3 has a 13th month observed starting Jan 16, 1154

Kiūju 1–2 Feb 14, 1154 to Jan 20, 1156

Hōgen 1–3 Jan 21, 1156 to Jan 20, 1159
Hōgen 1 has a 13th month observed starting Oct 16, 1156

Heiji 1 Jan 21, 1159 to Feb 8, 1160
Heiji 1 has a 13th month observed starting June 18, 1159

Eiriaku 1 Feb 9, 1160 to Jan 27, 1161

Ōhō 1–2 Jan 28, 1161 to Feb 4, 1163
Ōhō 2 has a 13th month observed starting April 17, 1162

Chōkwan 1–2 Feb 5, 1163 to Feb 12, 1165
Chōkwan 2 has a 13th month observed starting Dec 16, 1164

Eiman 1 Feb 13, 1165 – Feb 2, 1166

Nin-an 1–3 Feb 3, 1166 to Jan 29, 1169
Nin-an 2 has a 13th month observed starting August 17, 1167

Kaō 1–2 Jan 30, 1169 to Feb 6, 1171

Shōan 1–4 Feb 7, 1171 to Jan 23, 1175
Shōan 2 has a 13th month observed starting January 16, 1173

Angen 1–2 Jan 24, 1175 to Jan 31, 1177
Angen 1 has a 13th month observed starting October 17, 1175

JAPANESE HOURS

Hour	*Bell Strikes*	*Solar time*
Rabbit	6	5 – 7 AM
Dragon	5	7 – 9 AM
Snake	4	9 – 11 AM
Horse	9	11 AM – 1 PM *(Noon)*
Sheep	8	1 – 3 PM
Monkey	7	3 – 5 PM
Bird	6	5 – 7 PM
Dog – *Shokō, First Watch*	5	7 – 9 PM
Pig – *Nikō, Second Watch*	4	9 – 11 PM
Mouse – *Saukō, Third Watch*	9	11 PM – 1 AM *(Midnight)*
Ox – *Shikō, Fourth Watch*	8	1 – 3 AM *("witching hour")*
Tiger – *Gokō, Fifth Watch*	7	3 – 5 AM

NOTE: The hours of the day are defined as divisions of time between sunrise and sunset, and back to sunrise again. There are six Japanese hours in each day and six each night. The sun always rises in the Hour of the Rabbit, and sets in the Hour of the Bird. Naturally, as the seasons change, nighttime and daytime hours will vary in actual duration, daytime hours longer during the summer, nighttime hours longer during the winter. Averaged out over the year, each "hour" works out to be approximately two of our modern hours.

Acknowledgments

I want to thank my editor, Laura Lis Scott, for her indefatigable enthusiasm and support for this project. Her work not only with the manuscript, but in layout, cover design, historical research, and story development made a key difference in the final product.

I also would like to thank Tonia Hurst, Carolyn Burke, Anne Vonhof, and Stella Myers for their careful review of the early drafts and the final galleys, and their ardent support.

Thanks also goes to the beta readers for their insight and feedback, as well as their input in the cover art: Roslynn Pryor, Carolyn Studer, Janet Brantley and Crystal Thieringer. Finally I'd like to express my gratitude to Amy Bovaird, S.M. Larson, Lynn Ewback, Carryl A. Robinson, Vanessa von Mollendorf, and Rebecca Barth on their feedback on the cover design.

If you enjoyed Cold Blood

Please consider posting a brief review online
to help others discover the book.

Thank you!

Books by
Katherine M. Lawrence

Cold Saké

Sword of the Taka Samurai series

Cold Blood

Cold Rain

*Cold Heart**

*Cold Trail**

*Cold Fire**

*Cold Steel**

*Cold Fate**

** Coming soon*

About the Author

For several years, Katherine M. Lawrence has been researching and writing the adventures of Yamabuki, an actual historic female samurai who lived in the Heian Era of Japan. Inspired by several decades in the martial arts halls led by women—Ja Shin Do, the San Jose State University Kendo Club, and Pai Lum White Lotus Fist: Crane style—Katherine set out to write about the experiences of women who train in warriors' skills . . . and Yamabuki in particular.

Katherine graduated from the University of Washington with a BA degree in both History and Chemistry, and continued with work on a Masters in History at the Far Eastern and Slavic Institute. She also received an MBA from Harvard University.

She is currently developing further books about the adventures of Yamabuki. She lives in Boulder, Colorado.

Kate's blog: KateLore.com

Kate on Twitter: @pingkate

Kate's newsletter signup: eepurl.com/K8IIf

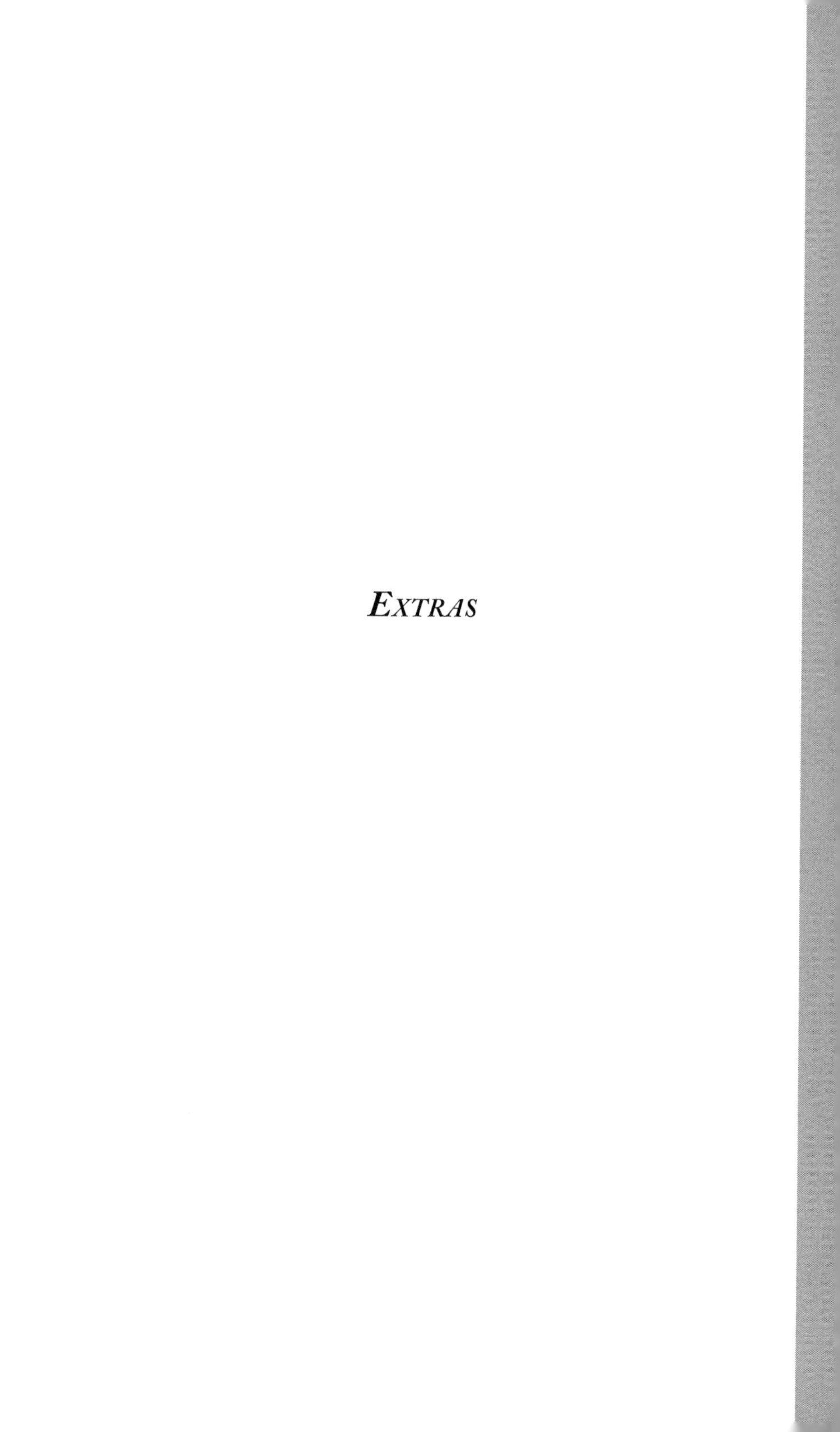

Extras

EXCERPT FROM COLD RAIN,
BOOK TWO OF
SWORD OF THE TAKA SAMURAI

The action of ***Cold Blood*** continues. . . .

Excerpt from Cold Rain:

One
Female Warriors Were Ordered to Beautify Themselves

Cold rain washed runnels of blood past her feet.

She had never been in an actual duel; never had anyone fallen before her sword. Three dead bodies lay in the road. Her palms still pulsed from the impact of steel against steel. The dying echoes of the assassins' screams lingered in her ears, mixing with the ever-increasing beat of the wind-driven rain. The skies turned black. Thunder rolled through the forest. The temperature dropped.

Even as icy showers drenched everything, she still felt flush. Rain soaked her hair. She mopped her brow. Cold entered her armor where her chest protector was torn. She touched her own breasts. The fencing master's blade had only split the corselet's outer layer. The imperial yellow under-silk remained intact. No blood. Not so much as a nick.

She wiped her cheek, fingering the single wound she received in the fray. It was viscid. Only when she touched it did it sting. Her naked fingertips extending from her sleeve-and-hand armor were now red. She let the *reiu* wash away the blood.

She had to get Mochizuki out of the ice storm. She took the colt's bridle, leading him to a sheltered place under the trees. His hot breath steamed. She looked into his dark-brown, moonlike eyes. "You never doubted I'd survive, did you?" Impassively the colt looked back at her.

Her breathing had almost returned to normal.

The rain and hail increased, drenching the dead, pelting them with pearl-white ice pebbles. The cloudburst grew so thick it became a fog. But like any fury, it abated. The rains began to die away. The grayness lifted. High clouds broke. The bright skies of noon shined through.

A piercing screech rose from the nearby Shintō shrine. A black kite perched on one of the crossbeams of the red *torii* entrance gate.

"A *tonbi*. Has he been watching us?"

Though usually not superstitious, she took comfort in the bird. A good omen. Kites were kin to *taka*. Taka: "hawk," her clan name.

The bird's gold-speckled eyes peered first at her, and then at the dead. As if agitated, it swiveled its head from side to side. Now left, then right, not able to make up its mind. It straightened itself. Shrieked. Then, beating its wings six or seven times, it flew up over the forest and soared into the blueness of the clearing sky. Giving forth a final prolonged and chilling cry, the tonbi disappeared.

"You know, Mochizuki, it's said kites carry fallen warriors' spirits into the next world." It was an ancient Taka clan belief—older than Shintō, going back to an age when spiritual matters were the province of female shamans. "The tonbi flew west," she said. "The Red Land lies beyond the setting sun."

The kite might possibly have flown off to the Western Paradise with the essences of the dead, but the bodies still lay where they fell. Though she had seen bodies before, until today she had never seen one decapitated.

Her father's retainers sometimes argued with an almost ghoulish relish, trying to sound jaundiced, about the fine points of "taking the head." A head was proof that a warlord's foe was truly dead.

An entire warrior lore had grown up around the "proper" way to cut off the head of a foe. It was an art. A head could not be allowed to putrefy. A bad smell was a breach of good manners. There were heated debates whether to use salt or saké as a preservative; salt dried out the face, but saké bloated the features.

The gruesome punctilios were sedulously followed by the Taka, not only in anticipation of victory but also in the case of their own deaths. Before a major battle, samurai were admonished to wash, oil, comb, and perfume their hair so that the smell of rotted flesh would not offend should their severed heads happen to be presented to their enemies. So that no one would suffer the humiliation of being taken for a girl, those whose facial hair was a fine fuzz were told to stain their beards and moustaches with darkening cream.

As for female warriors, they were ordered to beautify themselves.

Yamabuki imagined what might have happened had the assassins succeeded: Standing over her body, daggers drawn, they would be cutting her head away from her neck, ready to immerse it into some awful kill-box. She pictured her skull, dangling by its long black tresses, as the ninja lowered it into the liquid-filled canister. The saké, now tinged red by her blood, would slowly rise up under her chin, coming up to her gaping mouth and lips. As they lowered the head further, the liquid would move over her cheeks and cover her vacant eyes . . . until it closed around her forehead and her scalp as the last of her finally disappeared beneath the fluid. Only her hair would be left floating on the surface. And then the lid would be closed, sealing her in darkness.

Cold Rain is available now!

Excerpt from Cold Saké

Several months after the action of *Sword of the Taka Samurai* . . .

Alone deep in the wilderness, Yamabuki finds shelter at a forgotten inn. But before the night is out, she must fight for her life . . . and her sanity.

Available Now!

Excerpt from
Cold Saké

Last day before Gods Absent Month
Last day before Gods Absent Month
Five days after Dark Moon's Night
2nd Year of Shōan
October 31, 1172

The dusk promised rain. The rider knew it, the horse sensed it, the sky foretold it. Behind her, what remained of the day clung to an unsettled horizon of dirty orange, jade green, and deepening blue. Ahead of her, the rutted road snaked north-eastward—an unlucky direction.

The farmers back at Ogami village had assured her that she would reach East Wind Inn before sunset. Now it was past the Hour of the Monkey. She had ridden for over two hours without seeing so much as a hut.

Farmers! They'll say anything.

Near a washed-out bridge, the road detoured into a ravine where dead dry leaves danced about in small whirlwinds that carried with them the scent of autumn. She pulled her *jimbaori* cloak tighter, but still she shivered.

But then, as the road rose from the ravine, she spied a dark building in a shadowy grove of pines. A man stood near its entrance. "We may have arrived at last, Mochizuki," she whispered to her mount. Yet as she rode further, she saw that it was not an inn at all, but an abandoned Buddhist temple. Probably built to guard the northeast direction from an approach by demons, it had fallen into ruin, overgrown by vines; its gardens lay choked in dead grass; its ponds sat putrid and muddy.

What she had taken for a man at the entry turned out to be a statue of Jizō—patron and guardian of dead children's souls. Entangled among vines, one of his arms was lifted, reaching for what scant light fell into the wooded grove. Carved in gray stone, Jizō's compassionate eyes stared into the gloom, his chiseled, serene expression sending a smile to the lone traveler. His other hand remained outstretched in an attitude of blessing, his shattered fingers bearing mute witness to the statue's decay.

The rider eased out of her stirrup and swung down from the saddle. In the undergrowth, near a twisted pine tree, she found a round, black rock about the size of her fist, which she placed before Jizō. *A rock to help the dead children escape the Yellow Land.*

Mochizuki neighed nervously. "Why are you nickering?" But before she finished speaking, she saw two riders approaching through the twilight. Weapons sheathed, they rode toward her at a canter.

In a single motion she swung back into the saddle.

The strangers slowed to a trot. If they were brigands, their armor likely would be a hodgepodge of looted pieces; yet, both of these riders wore elegantly matched sets of armor.

Probably samurai.

But that didn't mean they weren't a threat.

She sat straight up in the saddle, paying attention to every subtlety.

The strangers brought their mounts to a halt.

"I am Shinjo Taro!" the elder warrior declared, raising his voice above the thump of hooves, pulling the woven blue silk cords of the bridle.

The comely one, the one who rode a half stride behind Taro, called out, "I am Sato Jiro!"

It was protocol for samurai to announce their names before a duel.

Do they seek combat?

"May we ask your name?" Taro's request was as much a command as it was anything.

"I am Taka Yamabuki!" she growled in answer as she had been taught, suppressing her female voice-range.

She eyed Taro—the dark and scarred one. His wild mane of hair could not conceal a grisly scar across his forehead. His forearms and face were likewise marked. Part of an ear was missing; two sword hand fingers, gone.

Fingers lost in battle, or forfeited for missteps?

Jiro looked at least ten years younger than Taro. For all of Taro's battle scars, Jiro was flawless and untouched.

Pretty.

He resembled a youthful courtier, or a young page; yet when their gazes met, she saw something icy and deadly lurking behind his eyes.

For a fleeting moment, she wondered if the two men were lovers. She knew that some warriors became emotionally drawn to one another. There was something about battle that forged these sorts of ties—deep ties. She pushed the thought aside. What they were to one another did not matter. She had to remain watchful. They were men; they were dangerous; and there were two of them.

Praise for Cold Saké

"I was thoroughly pleased with the portrayal and use of Yamabuki's gender as well—the story avoids the usual traps of the 'female warrior trope' by keeping Yamabuki human, indeed sometimes gloriously androgynous, yet the fact she is a woman is essential to the story."

—*A. Hurst*

"[I]t makes medieval Japan come alive."

—*Nina Wouk*

"Katherine Lawrence writes with a very strong sense of place, of time, and of character. Yamabuki rides alone . . . depending on her own wit and ability to survive."

—*Anne Vonhof*

"[T]he last time I remember anticipating a next novel in this way was way back when, awaiting delivery of the next in Robert Van Gulik's Judge Dee series."

—*Aptos*

About Toot Sweet Ink

Toot Sweet Ink is an imprint of Toot Sweet Inc., an independent publisher based in Boulder, Colorado.

Watch for our upcoming releases in historical fiction, science fiction, women's contemporary fiction, humor, and non-fiction—and more Yamabuki stories by Katherine M. Lawrence.

Website: TootSweetInk.com

Twitter: @TootSweetInk

Facebook: facebook.com/tootsweetink

Newsletter: Sign up to get updates and learn about new releases and discount opportunities on our upcoming titles at: eepurl.com/K8XVn